Donald MacKenzie and The Murder Room

>>> This title is part of The Murder Room, our series dedicated to making available out-of-print or hard-to-find titles by classic crime writers.

Crime fiction has always held up a mirror to society. The Victorians were fascinated by sensational murder and the emerging science of detection; now we are obsessed with the forensic detail of violent death. And no other genre has so captivated and enthralled readers.

Vast troves of classic crime writing have for a long time been unavailable to all but the most dedicated frequenters of second-hand bookshops. The advent of digital publishing means that we are now able to bring you the backlists of a huge range of titles by classic and contemporary crime writers, some of which have been out of print for decades.

From the genteel amateur private eyes of the Golden Age and the femmes fatales of pulp fiction, to the morally ambiguous hard-boiled detectives of mid twentieth-century America and their descendants who walk our twenty-first century streets, The Murder Room has it all. **>>>**

The Murder Room
Where Criminal Minds Me

themurderroom.com

T0352435

Donald MacKenzie 1908–1994

Donald MacKenzie was born in Ontario, Canada, and educated in England, Canada and Switzerland. For twenty-five years MacKenzie lived by crime in many countries. 'I went to jail,' he wrote, 'if not with depressing regularity, too often for my liking.' His last sentences were five years in the United States and three years in England, running consecutively. He began writing and selling stories when in American jail. 'I try to do exactly as I like as often as possible and I don't think I'm either psychopathic, a wayward boy, a problem of our time, a charming rogue. Or ever was.'

He had a wife, Estrela, and a daughter, and they divided their time between England, Portugal, Spain and Austria.

The Sixth Deadly Sin

Donald MacKenzie

An Orion book

Copyright © The Estate of Donald MacKenzie 1993

The right of Donald MacKenzie to be identified as the author of this work has been asserted in accordance with the Copyright, Designs and Patents Act 1988.

This edition published by
The Orion Publishing Group Ltd
Orion House
5 Upper St Martin's Lane
London WC2H 9EA

An Hachette UK company
A CIP catalogue record for this book is available from the British Library

ISBN 978 1 4719 0555 1

www.orionbooks.co.uk

For Bryan and Theresa Owram

Chapter One

Martin Mallory stopped the VW Passat in front of the wrought-iron gate blocking access to the driveway beyond. A man in dungarees was raking the grass behind the lodge. It had taken Mallory the best part of an hour to drive the twenty-six miles from London to Corton Bassett. He was thirty-four years old with thinning brown hair scraped back in a pony-tail tied with an elastic band. He was overweight for his modest height with anxious grey eyes pouched in flabby cheeks. He was wearing a brown tweed jacket with leather elbow-patches, corduroy trousers, chukka boots and a blue button-down tieless shirt.

He beeped the horn. The lodgekeeper dragged the gate back, his expression curious. Mallory wound his window down. 'You're not going to believe this, George. I got all the way home last night and discovered I'd left the bloody exam papers behind. I'm supposed to be marking them over the weekend.' He lectured twice a week at the Wycherly Foundation, Tuesdays and Thursdays. Today was Friday.

The lodgekeeper grunted. 'It's the memory cells. You ought to try tying a knot in your dick.'

The Passat bumped over the cattlegrid. The oak trees bordering the avenue were old and twisted, the barbed-wire fencing snagged with yellowing sheep wool. The recent rain had left the fields waterlogged. A board on the verge of the drive read:

1

WYCHERLY FOUNDATION FOR RELIGIOUS STUDIES
Principal: Ludovic Lambert MA (Edinburgh)
Registered Charity No: 29371

Mallory drove into the parking-space reserved for staff. Lucy Ashton's Fiesta stood in its usual place. It was a quarter past one on an overcast March afternoon. Lights burned in the long red-brick building in front of him.

The angle at which he was parked offered a partial view of the rear of the building. An array of scarred beech trees stretched down the slope to the river, the foliage partly concealing the two dormitories. There was one for each sex. The Wycherly maintained a liberal attitude to enrolment. There were no bars based upon race, religion or nationality. A working knowledge of English and the means to pay the fees were all that was necessary. Once accepted, a few selected students might be transferred to one or other of the sister institutions in Germany or France. The full complement of pupils numbered one hundred and fifty, approximately half male and half female. There were eighteen full-time teachers and an administration staff of twelve. Most of these lived in the neighbouring villages.

Mallory owned a small flat at the top of a mansion-block in Chelsea. He earned enough money to support his modest lifestyle. His pleasures were simple. He read a great deal, listened to music and saw the occasional film or play. He spent three Saturdays a month as a voluntary prison visitor and supported the Green Party's political aims. His sexual adventures were infrequent. He blamed this on the difficulty of meeting the right sort of woman. All this had changed dramatically two months ago. He had been reading the roster of newly inducted students, people rising in turn to answer their names. He found it impossible to ignore the girl sitting immediately below the podium. Li Cho was a twenty-two-year-old from Kowloon, slight and delicately boned and dressed in a bright yellow top and matching trousers. Glossy black hair fell to her shoulders. She occupied the same seat at each subsequent lecture. Mallory's interest grew as the course continued. Foundation policy discouraged undue familiarity between staff and students but Mallory found an excuse to talk to the girl at the end of a lecture-period. He asked if she ever came to London. She studied his face for a moment. Her laugh sounded like tinkling glass. She wanted to know why he had taken so long to ask her. He watched her go with a feeling of incredulity. There'd been no guile in her manner, no flirtatiousness. Just an acceptance of something inevitable.

Students applying for weekend exeats made their requests to Lucy Ashton, the Principal's personal assistant. Li Cho invented a Kowloon family living in London and took a train to Waterloo every Friday evening. She returned to the Wycherly on Sunday, spending the two nights with Mallory. At the end of six weeks he was obsessed with her, happier than he had ever thought possible. A romantic at heart, he was thinking of marriage. The idyll ended as unexpectedly as it had begun. Mallory turned up as usual for his Tuesday lecture to find that Li Cho's name had been erased from his register. The next few hours were hard to endure. No one else in the class appeared to know where she was. The Bursar's assistant told Mallory that Li Cho had been transferred. Any further enquiries should be addressed to the Principal.

Mallory finished the day bereft and uncertain. He refused to believe that Li would have gone without getting in touch with him. His doubts hardened into resentful suspicion. Someone was keeping them apart, he was sure of it. The following Thursday he found an envelope addressed to him in the staff mailbox. It was from Lucy Ashton, inviting him to come to her cottage before he returned to London. Lucy said that she knew of his concern for Li Cho. She had gone through the same sort of experience herself, she confided, and told him of her affair with Ludovic Lambert. He had betrayed her trust and she no longer owed him loyalty. Convinced by her vehemence, Mallory opened his heart to her. She proved a sympathetic and knowledgeable listener. She told him that his girlfriend had probably been moved to Germany. The details of any such transfers were confidential. But if Mallory pledged himself to secrecy she would help him establish the truth about Li Cho. He had left her cottage buoyed on hope. Since then their only contact had been by telephone. She had called him two days before with her final instructions.

Mallory mounted the wide staircase that gave access to the upper storey and tapped on the door to the Principal's study. It was a large room with four windows hung with bronze velvet curtains and jade-coloured walls devoid of ornament. Diffused ceiling lighting illuminated an elegant desk and well-stocked bookcases. Bokhara rugs glowed on the polished parquet.

Lucy Ashton reclined on a low sofa. She was thirty-four years old with ash-blonde hair cut in a modish bob. Her skin had the unhealthy hue of egg-white. She was wearing a loose-fitting apple green shirt over a camel-hair skirt. Her slim legs tapered into sensible country shoes. She looked at him worriedly, contact lenses correcting her short-sightedness.

'Did anyone notice you?'

He lowered himself beside her. 'Only George on the gate. I told him I'd forgotten some papers.'

'Then we'd better make this quick,' she said. 'Lambert took the transfer list to London. Herr Liedemann's flying in from Düsseldorf. They're meeting tomorrow afternoon. Hollywood Mews will be empty tonight.'

'We've got to be sure,' Mallory insisted.

She pulled a newspaper clipping from her handbag. The photograph featured a man and a woman raising their glasses to the camera. The woman's gown plunged to her cleavage, her hair cascading over bare shoulders. The man standing next to her had a full head of white hair and a well-tailored evening suit. The camera had caught him smiling. The caption below identified the couple.

Mrs Isobel Ballantyne and Mr Ludovic Lambert
at the ball given in aid of the Wycherly Foundation.

Mallory surrendered the clipping. 'Who's the lady?'

'That's his latest,' said Lucy with a moue of distaste. 'Her husband divorced her eight months ago. Ludo's been having an affair with her. That's where he'll be spending the night.

'I *know* the way he operates. I see his credit-card statements, remember, the bills for the flowers and perfume. It may not last much longer but you can be sure that he'll get his money's worth.'

He found himself disturbed by her bitterness. 'Why wouldn't he take the transfer list with him?'

She looked at him, shaking her head. 'Because that's the way he reasons. He's devious, Martin. He's the only one who sees the list. He even types it himself. He just wouldn't run the risk. He'll lock it away in the safe overnight and pick it up on his way to meet Liedemann tomorrow. Believe me, I know how his mind works. I'm worried about this friend of yours.'

'There's no reason for that,' he replied.

'A man who's just come out of prison,' she challenged. 'How do you know he can be trusted?'

'Nick's doing this as a friend,' said Mallory. 'I told him about Li Cho and the safe and he offered to help me.'

'That's what disturbs me,' she answered. 'Why would a man in his situation do something like this for a stranger?'

'I'm not a stranger,' he replied. 'You don't seem to understand this relationship. Nick's wife took off the moment he was sentenced. He didn't get any letters or visits. I was his only link with the outside world for two years. People bond in those circumstances, Lucy. He's genuinely concerned for me.'

She niggled away like an aching tooth. 'To the point of breaking the law?'

'That's right,' he agreed. 'He's the one who suggested it. He said that I needed professional help. I don't see your problem.'

She peered at him suspiciously. 'Does he know where you're getting the keys?'

Her insistence was beginning to get to him. 'I didn't mention your name, if that's what you mean. He knows where I work. You don't have to go into details with someone like Nick. They wouldn't concern him. We've gone over this before. You're the one who's creating the difficulties.'

'I'm sorry,' she said. 'But I can't help the way I feel.'

'It was your idea in the first place,' he reminded her. 'Have you got the keys?'

She dipped into her handbag again and gave him two house keys on a ring. The third was a slim double-warded safe key. He looked at it; then the keys chinked in his jacket pocket. 'What about the cleaner you mentioned?'

Her slim fingers gestured indifferently. 'She doesn't come in when Ludo's in London. He's paranoiac about people knowing his business. The thing is, I've got to have those keys back before he realizes that the house has been burgled. I'm having supper with Annie Ridler tonight. It's something we do every Friday. One week at her place, the next week at mine. It's her turn tonight which means that I won't be home before eleven o'clock at the earliest.'

'Don't worry,' he said. 'They'll be there when you get back. I'll drop them through your cat flap.'

She looked at her watch and rose. 'You'd better go,' she urged. 'I don't want the girls from Admin to see you up here.'

For a moment he thought she was going to embrace him. But the touch of her fingers was as light as a leaf on his sleeve.

'Be careful,' she counselled.

He met no one on his way down the stairs. He unlocked his desk in the lecture-room and removed a sheaf of examination papers, an excuse for his unscheduled visit. Deceit had never been part of his nature and he found the prospect disturbing.

He took less than an hour to drive back to Elm Park Mansions. He left his car in front of the church and entered the old-fashioned mansion-block. The hallway was bleak and forbidding. He climbed the uncarpeted stairs to the top floor and let himself into his flat. A divan faced the gingham-curtained windows in his bedroom. There was a framed picture of Li Cho on a shelf. An Olivetti portable typewriter lay on the card-table in front of the wardrobe. The small bathroom had a flush toilet under the frosted-glass panes. The kitchen next door was no larger. A large storage closet backed a flat vinyl work surface. An oil-fired boiler in the basement provided the communal heating.

Mallory spent most of his time in the sitting-room. A three-seater sofa was positioned in front of the television set. Beanbags offered the only alternative vantage point. There was a telephone and an answering-machine on a side-table, Picasso prints on the walls. A couple of high-fidelity speakers were attached to a Sanyo music centre. Mallory put the examination papers in his desk and dropped his duffle-coat on the floor.

Prison visitors were always given the case-reports on inmates before placing the names on their lists. Nick Berry's sheet had proved instructive. He had virtually lived on the streets from the age of fifteen, pilfering unattended goods from the backs of delivery vans. The report on him cited his first arrest for stealing by means of a trick. The magistrate suspended his sentence. There was no record of the following few years. Nick's next known offence appeared to be fortuitous, the result of a summer evening stroll through Pimlico. He had noticed scaffolding erected outside a mansion-block. His reaction had been impulsive. He scaled the scaffolding and stepped through an open window into a flat left temporarily empty. A quick search of a bedroom drawer netted an album of postage stamps. Each page was conveniently catalogued and resulted in a total of twenty-eight thousand pounds. Nick left the flat by the front door as the owner emerged from the lift. Nick offered no resistance and a squad car arrived minutes later. A check on Nick's file at the CRO revealed his previous arrest. A Crown Court judge with Victorian values passed a sentence of three years' imprisonment.

Mallory had visited him faithfully over the months that followed, intrigued by Nick's personality. Nick had explained his views about friendship. There were three things you needed to trust a man with before you could call him a real friend: your woman, your money and your liberty. The last was the most important. Without your freedom the other two were meaningless. It was an aspect of life that was new to Mallory. He wondered how he fitted into the equation.

The door-buzzer sounded three times in quick succession. Mallory released the entrance door below and waited outside on the landing for Nick to appear. He was a thirty-year-old South Londoner with sandy hair and a friendly grin, his face still pinched in prison pallor. He was wearing the grey suit that Mallory had given him, a pair of rubber-soled shoes and a see-through nylon slicker. He lowered himself gingerly on to a beanbag and winced.

'Them stairs is a bleedin' killer, mate. You got to be a lot fitter than you look.'

'You get used to them,' said Mallory. 'Have you been to the house?'

'I just come from there,' said Nick. 'You didn't say nothing about the burglar alarm.'

'It isn't working,' said Mallory. 'It kept going off in the night and the neighbours complained.'

Nick held out his hand. 'Have you got the keys?'

Mallory felt in his pockets. It was the safe key that seemed to interest Nick most. 'Are you sure this is all? No combination or nothing like that?'

Mallory found Nick's expertise reassuring. 'Just what you see there. I've got to have the keys back straight away. How long do you think it'll take?'

'It should be a doddle,' said Nick. 'In and out like the milkman. I'd say ten minutes tops. Is there anything else in the safe – no little souvenirs?'

'I wouldn't think so,' said Mallory. 'The owner's in the country most of the time. He only comes up to London occasionally.'

'Funny old world, isn't it?' Nick said reflectively. 'Me and you sitting here talking about screwing somebody's gaff. I like it.'

'You seem to be treating the whole thing like some sort of joke,' said Mallory.

Nick cocked his head. 'You sound like that old fart who sentenced me. I'm just helping a friend, mate. What's wrong with that?'

'As long as it doesn't become a habit,' said Mallory.

'It won't,' said Nick, pocketing the keys. 'I've got other ways of making a living. You'd better give the house a bell.'

Mallory dialled the number. It rang for a while unanswered. 'There's nobody there,' he said.

Nick struggled up from the beanbag. 'Let's get it over and done with.'

They descended the five flights of stone stairs to the shadowed street. Mallory unlocked the Passat. Nick took the passenger seat next to him and pulled a pair of surgical gloves from his pocket. He blew the chalk from the latex and smoothed each finger carefully. The light from the street-lamp fell across the back of his shoulders, leaving his face curious.

'I was thinking – what happens if it turns out this chick don't want to know you no more?'

Mallory tapped the fuel gauge. There was enough petrol to get him to Corton Bassett and back without having to stop at a filling-station. 'That's a sad and depressing thought,' he said, 'and one that I refuse to consider.'

'Me and my big mouth,' Nick answered quickly. 'It's always getting me into trouble. I'm sorry.'

'Forget it,' said Mallory. 'Some of us are just luckier than others. You'll understand when you meet her.' He knew too well what had prompted the question. Nick's experience with his wife had destroyed whatever faith he had had in women.

Mallory set the car in motion and drove across Fulham Road, then left on to Priory Walk. Hollywood Mews was a hundred-yard stretch of small elegant homes built in varying styles with garages. A double yellow line painted on each side of the cobblestones signalled no waiting or stopping. A glimmer of light showed behind a yellow door on the left.

Nick's voice was knowing. 'That wasn't on earlier, it's a time switch to scare off people like us. Don't worry about it.'

Mallory turned off the motor and nodded across at a first-floor window. 'That's the bedroom.'

Nick closed the passenger door quietly and crossed the glistening cobblestones with the confident gait of a man going about his lawful occupation. He inserted the mortice key in the lower lock and met no resistance. The Yale key let him into a long narrow hallway smelling of furniture polish. A gilt-framed mirror reflected a short flight of thickly carpeted stairs opposite. A few letters addressed to Ludovic Lambert lay on the hallway table. He paused with his hand on the banister, listening to the drone of an airplane starting its descent to Heathrow. He climbed the stairs to the floor above. The door on his left was ajar, the bedroom in darkness. His gloved fingers felt for the switch. A light came on, illuminating the neatly made bed and winged dressing-table. There was the same smell of lavender furniture polish. No attempt had been made to conceal the small square safe set waist-high in the wall next to the wardrobe. He lifted the brass cover protecting the lock and inserted the double-warded key. He rotated his wrist. The safe door swung open, revealing a manila folder on the top shelf. He stuffed the folder into his jacket pocket, relocked the safe and glanced at the seven-day alarm clock next to the white telephone on the bedside table. He extinguished the light with a quick flash of satisfaction. He had been in the house less than five minutes.

He was halfway down the stairs when a fat woman wearing a pinafore came out of a door at the end of the hallway. She stared up at him with unfocused eyes, clinging to the wall for support. She lurched forward belligerently.

'What do you think you're doing?' she demanded. 'Who are you?'

He pushed past her and wrenched the front door open. His feet hit the cobblestones, running. He heard her shout, then the door slammed. There was no sign of alarm in the neighbouring houses. His exit had passed unnoticed.

Mallory was holding the passenger door open, his face taut with alarm.

'What happened?'

Nick thrust the manila folder at him. 'Just get this fucking thing moving,' he gasped. He stripped the gloves from his fingers, his face set in anger. A couple of seconds earlier and he would have been trapped.

The traffic-lights on Fulham Road were green. Mallory swung right then left on to Limerston Street.

Nick found his voice again as they neared Camera Place. 'Pull over,' he ordered.

The front wheels hit the kerb and the car stopped. Both men took their eyes from the rear-view mirror. 'I'll tell you what happened,' said Nick. 'I was halfway down the stairs when this woman come out of the kitchen or somewhere. She was pissed out of her mind but she got a good look at me.'

Mallory closed his eyes. 'You didn't hit her, I hope?'

'I didn't lay a finger on her,' Nick said. The memory lit a fire in his brain. 'She was as close to me as you are. I could have been nicked, for crissakes!'

'It's got to be the cleaner,' Mallory said quickly. 'I don't understand. She wasn't even supposed to be there.'

Nick spoke with hard resentment. 'That's what you get for working with mugs, Martin.'

Mallory laid a consoling hand on Nick's knee. 'Take a deep breath and relax,' he counselled. 'I'm sure it's not as bad as it sounds. As far as she knows there's nothing missing. Not only that, she's been at Lambert's booze. The last thing she'll want to do is call the police. I mean, there's no point to it. Don't you see that? She's going to get out of that house as fast as you did. She won't even want to remember it happened.'

'You think so?' said Nick.

Mallory removed his hand from Nick's knee. 'I'm sure of it.'

Nick thought for a moment, then a hint of a smile brightened his face. 'You always did have a way with words. But I'll tell you one thing, mate. Whoever gave you that information's a real piss artist.'

Mallory tapped the manila folder. 'I've learned one thing at any rate. I know what you mean about friendship.'

Nick's smile was broad now, his cocky resilience completely restored.

'As long as you don't spring no more of these dodgy capers on me.' His eyes sought the rear-view mirror again. 'I think I'll go home and have a few pints. That woman's breath give me the flavour.' He opened the door and leaned back. 'Let this be a lesson to you, mate. Thieving ain't always as easy as it looks. I'll give you a bell tomorrow.'

Mallory watched him as far as the King's Road and

held the two pages of closely spaced typescript under the light from the dashboard. His hope sank when he saw the meaningless entries of initials and digits. Maybe Lucy could shed some enlightenment. Discretion warned him not to leave a note with the keys that Nick had returned. He'd just have to wait until she called him.

It was half-past nine when he drove into Lucy's empty car port. The television was playing in the cottage next door. He dropped the three keys through the cat flap in the kitchen door and made good time back to London. He let himself into his flat, drained and exhausted. He locked the manila folder in his desk and carried a glass of brandy into the bedroom. He'd spent his whole life listening to people extol the importance of applied wisdom. The truth was that philosophy had no place in the world he'd just joined. This was the time for action.

Chapter Two

Ludovic Lambert closed Isobel Ballantyne's bedroom door quietly and tiptoed along the corridor to the bathroom. He used the razor and toothbrush he kept in the medicine chest and put his clothes on in the dressing-room. He carried his shoes down the stairs to the kitchen, made himself coffee and stood looking out of the window. It had rained during the night. Puddles had formed along the edges of the driveway. The Bentley Continental glistened like a roach under the dripping trees. He let himself out through the front door without a backward glance at Isobel Ballantyne's window.

On a good day Lambert could pass himself off as forty-eight, knocking ten years off his real age. His white hair was premature, he explained, the result of a bout of rheumatic fever. Good bone structure and an air of restrained virility added credence to the story. But today was a bad day. He had drunk too much and Isobel had been argumentative. She was becoming increasingly demanding. He'd already decided to ease himself out of the relationship. He'd have to be careful. Isobel was responsible for introducing several generous donors to the Wycherly Foundation.

He angled the driving-mirror, assessing his appearance. He was wearing a grey Huntsman suit, black handmade shoes and a Patek Philippe watch on a snakeskin strap. It was an image that he hoped Herr Liedemann would appreciate.

He had a quick run into London. It was Saturday and most of his neighbours spent the weekends in the country. The Wycherly Foundation owned the small house. It was used to entertain visitors from overseas. Other than himself, Lucy Ashton was the only person who had slept there. He thought of her now with indulgence. The way she had taken the end of their affair had surprised him. There'd been no bitterness, none of the recriminations he'd expected. They'd had their good times together, she said. What they had to do now was stay friends and get on with their lives. She'd continue her job if that was what he wanted and give him the same loyalty she had always done. Lambert accepted the offer gladly. Lucy had been with him for more than five years. It would have been difficult to replace her. Their relationship remained close, with the no-go areas clearly defined. Isobel Ballantyne would be harder to handle.

Liedemann's plane was due in at four o'clock. Their meeting would occupy no more than half an hour. The German was taking the next flight back to Düsseldorf. Lambert's plan was to drive straight on down to the country.

He let himself into the silent house and draped his cashmere overcoat over the banisters. There was a note addressed to him on the hallway table.

Reference the break-in at your premises. Please contact Chelsea Police Station, 2 Lucan Place, SW3, 081–741 6212 Det-Sergeant Fraser CID.

Lambert's immediate thought was the safe. He ran up the stairs. At first glance the bedroom looked as he had left it the previous morning. He unlocked the safe with foreboding and saw that the manila folder had gone. The implications spread through his brain like a virus. He relocked the safe and used the phone.

'This is Ludovic Lambert,' he said. 'I found your note.'

'Hang on a minute.' There was a rustle of papers at the other end. 'Where are you speaking from, sir?'

'I'm at home,' said Lambert. 'Look, I spent the night with some friends in Greenwich. I only got back a few minutes ago. I've looked through the house. There doesn't seem to be any sign of a break-in. As far as I can see, nothing is missing.'

'I think you'd better come round to the station, sir. Can you do that?'

'I'll be there as soon as I can,' said Lambert.

He redialled and waited. A woman responded. 'Wycherly Foundation, Hohen Limburg.'

'Ludovic Lambert speaking,' he said in English. 'Let me talk to Herr Liedemann, please.'

'I am sorry,' she said. 'Herr Liedemann has not yet arrived at the office. May I take a message?'

'I'm supposed to be meeting him at Heathrow this afternoon.'

'I have his ticket in front of me,' she said. 'Herr Liedemann is collecting it later.'

'You'll have to cancel it,' Lambert instructed. 'Something came up unexpectedly. Give my regrets to Herr Liedemann and say I'll call him as soon as possible.'

Her voice was brisk and businesslike. 'I'll tell him the moment he comes in, Mister Lambert. Thank you for calling.'

Lambert replaced the phone. Chelsea Police Station was a fifteen-minute walk. He needed time to compose his thoughts. He opened the front door. He breathed in deeply every six paces, filling his lungs. Then the same thing, breathing out. His heart rate had slowed when he reached Lucan Place. A breast-high counter bisected the reception area. A uniformed sergeant leaned on an elbow.

'Good morning, sir. What can we do for you?'

'Will you tell Detective-Sergeant Fraser that Ludovic Lambert is here?'

The desk-sergeant smiled. 'The waiting-room's on the left. I'll let him know that you're here.'

Lambert walked past WANTED posters, an appeal for blood donors, a warning to the public to be alert for any suspicious packages. The interview-room was meagrely furnished with a plain deal table and two straight-backed chairs. Lambert took one of them. The calendar on the wall bore the name of a firm of handcuff-makers. The windows were frosted, the floor covered with burn-scarred linoleum. The door opened.

Detective-Sergeant Fraser was a balding thirty-year-old wearing a baggy brown suit and the look of a man who would rather be somewhere else. He kicked the door shut and sat on the opposite side of the table. He took out a notebook and glanced at it briefly.

'Now, sir. I understand that you work for the Wycherly Foundation in Corton Bassett. Is that correct?'

'I'm the Principal,' Lambert said stiffly.

'So which is your home address, sir – Hollywood Mews or Corton Bassett?'

'I've never really thought about it,' said Lambert. 'Is it important?'

The detective-sergeant had the touchy manner of someone in need of sleep. 'Any questions I ask are important, sir.'

Lambert shed some of his composure. 'Then we'd better say Corton Bassett.'

'Do you own the house in Hollywood Mews, Mister Lambert?'

'No, the Foundation does. We use it to entertain overseas visitors. I'm not there very often.'

Fraser scribbled a note in his pad. 'About last night, sir. You say you stayed with some friends in Greenwich. Is that your normal procedure when you come to London?'

'Not really. This was a special occasion.'

'And you employ a cleaner – is that correct, sir?'

'There's a woman who comes in three times a week to keep an eye on things.'

'Was she there yesterday?'

'I've no idea,' said Lambert. 'There are no specified

days. She has other work in the area and chooses her own times.'

Fraser leaned back, turning his pen between finger and thumb.

'But she didn't get in touch with you yesterday?'

'No.'

'What about security?'

Lambert lifted a shoulder. 'There's no way of getting in from the back, if that's what you mean. The kitchen windows are fitted with anti-burglar devices. The locks on the front door are adequate.'

'So you had no idea that your house had been burgled until this morning?'

'None at all,' replied Lambert. 'Not until I found your note. I wasn't even sure what it meant. There are some valuables in the sitting-room but nothing down there was missing. I saw no sign of a break-in.'

Fraser consulted his notebook again. His voice assumed a sort of stiff formality.

'A female made a 999 call at 1830 hours yesterday. She identified herself as a Mrs Slater, the cleaner at 86 Hollywood Close. She stated that she had seen an intruder coming down the stairs from the bedroom. I attended the scene in the company of another officer. Mrs Slater let us in. We made an immediate search of the premises but found no trace of the alleged intruder. There were no indications of a forced entry.'

'That's what I wondered about,' said Lambert.

'What about the safe in the bedroom?'

Lambert shook his head. 'It's empty. We never keep anything in it. And the burglar alarm's been off for a year. We were getting too many complaints about it. You know, going off in the middle of the night and so forth.'

Fraser extended his arms, yawned and shivered. 'Mrs Slater has her own keys, I take it. Are there any others?'

'Only mine. There's a spare set we keep down in the country and that's all.'

Fraser wiped bloodshot eyes. 'Mrs Slater's a drinker. She was drunk when we got there. She stank like a brewery. If she'd been on the street I'd have nicked her. She couldn't even give a coherent description of the man she had seen.'

'Good God,' Lambert said, sitting up straight. 'I'd no idea that she drank.'

'Take my word for it, sir.' He snapped the rubber band on his notebook and blocked another yawn. 'Do you still want to make a complaint, sir?'

'What do you suggest?' asked Lambert.

'It's up to you,' said Fraser. 'According to you, there's nothing missing. My advice is to get rid of your cleaner and have your front-door locks changed. As I say, the decision is yours. But if you do want to go through with it you may have some trouble with your insurance company.'

Lambert rose to his feet. 'I'll take your advice. I'm sorry we've caused so much trouble. And thanks for your help.'

Lambert walked back to Hollywood Mews and wrote a note of dismissal to Mrs Slater enclosing a cheque for a month's wages. Then he called a twenty-four-hour service and arranged for the locks to be changed. He told them to send the keys to Corton Bassett and went out to the Bentley. Once on the Portsmouth road, he drove in the slow lane, his mind on the robbery. A single error of judgement had placed his future at risk. The thief's identity troubled him no less than his purpose. Lambert's business with Liedemann was never discussed on the telephone. He'd typed the papers himself. Yet someone had known where they were and removed them.

He took the exit to Corton Bassett. It was Saturday and the red-brick building was deserted until Monday morning. Students who stayed on campus made their own arrangements for eating. He let himself into the entrance hall, dropped the letter to the cleaner in the postbox and went upstairs to the administration offices. Lucy Ashton's desk displayed its usual neatness. A tray of outgoing letters awaited his signature. He opened the drawer where the spare set of keys was kept. They lay in their usual place. He went next door to his study and stood at the window. Mist from the river obscured the dormitories. A sentinel crown rose from a weathervane. Nothing else moved in the total stillness.

He left the grounds through the back gate and drove through Corton Bassett into a lane sunk deep between hawthorn hedges. The two thatched cottages stood side by side. Smoke wreathed from both chimneys. Lucy Ashton's Fiesta was parked in the carport. He left the Bentley in front of it. The front door opened as he approached. Lucy peered out. She was wearing her usual weekend attire: a black shapeless sweater, a skirt and a pair of dirty tennis shoes.

Her voice was surprised. 'Why didn't you tell me you were coming?'

There was a bag of groceries on the kitchen table, underclothes on the ironing-board. He pushed by without answering and slumped on the sofa in front of the fire.

She followed him into the sitting-room, her face concerned.

'You don't look well, Ludo. What's happened?'

He drew her down on the sofa beside him. 'You've got to promise you won't say a word to anyone else.'

'Of course,' she said quickly. 'What is it, for God's sake?'

'The worst,' he said grimly. 'You know I was supposed to see Liedemann today?'

She nodded.

'I took some confidential papers with me to London. I left them in the safe overnight. They were gone when I got back to the mews this morning.'

Her fingers flew to her throat. 'You mean *stolen*?'

'Stolen,' he said. 'Those papers contained details of money given to the Foundation by donors with their own

20

reasons for wanting to remain anonymous. I have to respect their wishes. If the Charity Commissioners ever got wind of it, all hell would break loose. I'd be finished professionally.'

Her face was a mask of bafflement. 'But how could you *do* something like that? You of all people!'

He turned his head towards her. 'I've never been good at lying to you, Lucy. I spent the night at Isobel Ballantyne's house in Greenwich.'

She smiled. 'You and I made a pact, remember. It's not my concern any more who you sleep with.'

'I know that. But I'm trying to explain how this happened. Have you any idea how much money goes through our external account in a year?'

'I don't see the figures,' she answered.

'Close to a million pounds free of tax. Liedemann handles everything.'

Her voice warmed with sympathy. 'What a terrible, terrible mess. Poor Ludo.'

'I've had to put Liedemann off,' he continued. 'I don't want to get into explaining what's happened until I've had time to reflect.'

'Have you any idea who could have done it?'

'If I knew I wouldn't be sitting here,' he said. 'But whoever it was must have been looking for something else.'

'But how did the thief get into the house?' Lucy demanded. 'The spare keys never leave my desk.'

'I'm getting to that,' he replied. 'When I got back to the house this morning I found a note from the police asking me to contact Chelsea Police Station. I went round there and talked to a CID sergeant. It turns out that Mrs Slater was in the house yesterday evening. She saw a man coming down the stairs and called 999.'

Lucy's brain seemed to have been anaesthetized. 'Was she hurt?'

'She was drunk,' said Lambert. 'According to the officer

she could barely make sense, let alone describe the man she's supposed to have seen. The police weren't too happy about the incident. I didn't tell them that the safe had been opened, for obvious reasons. I can't run the risk. Anyway, the officer suggested that since nothing was missing the best thing for me to do was get the front-door locks changed and sack Mrs Slater. And that's what I've done.'

She hunkered down in front of the fireplace and poked flame from the logs. She wiped her hands on her skirt and sat down beside him again.

'The point is,' he said, 'those papers won't mean a thing to whoever stole them. He'll probably throw them away, destroy them.'

'Then it can't be as bad as all that,' she said. 'You must have a copy somewhere.'

He shook his head. 'I didn't make any copies. I just couldn't take the chance.'

Her voice was gentle. 'If there's anything that I can do to help, anything at all, all you need to do is tell me.'

His eyes searched her face. 'The biggest mistake I ever made was letting you go. I never felt so alone in my life.'

'You're *not* alone,' she said quickly. 'I'm still here. I'm glad that you told me the truth. Two heads are always better than one, remember. We've got to think things through very carefully. Get some sort of sense of direction. You can rely on me to say nothing to anyone else, you know that, Ludo.'

He drew a deep breath of relief. 'You've given me the strength I needed. We'll sleep on it. One of us might well come up with the right solution.' He put his cheek against hers and held her tight for a moment. 'You're a true friend. We'll talk tomorrow.'

She watched from the window until the Bentley was out of sight in the fading light. She drew the curtains and resumed her ironing. Her eyes were stinging by the time she had finished. She dismantled the board and went

22

upstairs to the bathroom. She washed her hands in the basin and placed a clean linen towel on the vanity unit. She leaned over the towel and lifted the top lid of her right eye with her left index finger, drawing the lower lid sideways with her middle right finger. The contact lens slipped on to the face-towel. She repeated the process with the other eye and placed both lenses in a bowl of cleansing solution.

She went into her bedroom and opened a drawer in the dressing-table. She took out the box that contained her personal papers.

She was not deceived by Lambert's display of helplessness. She knew only too well his ability to hide his true feelings. She sensed his stealthy approach to her secret. One thing was certain. He was deeply concerned by the loss of his papers. What she had to do now was continue to play the part of the loyal friend. That and keep Mallory from panicking.

She looked in the box. Her passport was valid for three more years. Her deposit account showed a credit balance of £17,428. There were plenty of opportunities for jobs in one of the EC organizations. Somewhere like Strasbourg or Brussels. Her French was good and she had the right kind of qualifications. There was nothing to hold her in England now that her purpose had been achieved.

The sitting-room was warm and snug. She lifted the telephone and heard the familiar sound of Chopin on Mallory's answering-machine. She spoke clearly.

'Call me the moment you're home. It's important.'

She dragged the television nearer so that she could see the screen, curled up on the sofa and watched an old Bogart movie.

A car drew up in the lane outside. Her first thought was that Lambert was back. She went into the hallway and unlocked the front door.

Two men were standing outside. The one in front looked about forty with curly brown hair. He was wearing a long dark raincoat. He showed her a plasticized warrant-card.

'Detective-Inspector Bellamy, miss.' He jerked a hand at his partner. 'Detective-Sergeant Wainwright.'

The younger man was dressed in a black leather jacket. He had pale-blue eyes and a flattened nose. He made no acknowledgement. Lucy disliked him on sight and continued to block the doorway.

Bellamy peered into the hallway. 'Are you Miss Lucy Ashton?'

'That's right,' she agreed.

'Do you mind if we come in for a moment, miss? It won't take long.'

The two men wiped their feet on the doormat and followed her into the sitting-room.

Bellamy looked at the fire with approval. 'Nothing like apple logs for burning. They smell good and it discourages earwigs.'

His partner turned off the television set and stood near the writing-bureau.

'Do you mind telling me why you're here, Inspector?' Lucy asked.

Bellamy lowered himself on to the sofa and covered his knees with his hands. 'Of course, miss. We're from Chelsea CID. We shouldn't even be here by rights. But it's an odd situation. I understand you work for Mister Lambert at the Wycherly Foundation.'

She tried hard to hide her anxiety. 'I'm his personal assistant.'

'Then you know about the burglary in Hollywood Mews, miss?'

'Mister Lambert told me a couple of hours ago.'

'He's got some strange ideas about security. I mean, a house with valuable possessions left in the charge of a drunken woman. I wouldn't call that very sensible.'

'I understood that nothing was stolen,' said Lucy. She turned her head sharply. The younger man had left the

24

room. She heard the stairs creak as he went upstairs.

'He's got a weak bladder,' Bellamy said. 'Don't worry about it.'

The phone shrilled before she could comment. She ignored the ringing. She knew who was calling.

'Aren't you going to answer that, miss?' said Bellamy.

She lifted the phone and spoke with her back to him. 'Three four six.'

Mallory's voice sounded worried. 'I just this moment got in. I'm sorry.'

'I can't talk to you now,' she said urgently. 'I've got someone here. I'll call you back later.'

She put the phone down and resumed her seat on the sofa. 'I'm sorry. You were talking about the burglary.'

'That's right, miss, we were.' Bellamy put an arm along the back of the sofa. 'We need your co-operation, Miss Ashton. We're dealing with a series of similar crimes in Chelsea and Fulham. Some of those involve large sums of money. The owners weren't as lucky as Mister Lambert. We're holding a man in custody we think is responsible. I believe that a spare set of keys to Hollywood Mews is kept in your office.'

The cistern flushed in the bathroom. The detective-sergeant returned to the room.

'Those keys never leave my desk,' she said steadily.

Wainwright spoke for the first time. His tone matched his eyes, flat and accusing. 'How do you know that?'

Bellamy frowned. 'Why don't you go out and wait in the car?' he suggested.

The front door opened and shut.

'He's a good officer,' said Bellamy. 'He's just not used to dealing with ladies. I'll put my cards on the table, Miss Ashton. We think there's a chance that the man we're holding might have been down to Corton Bassett, taken an impression of the keys in your desk.'

'That's ridiculous. There's always someone there in the office.'

'I'm talking about during the night, miss. It's the way these people operate. They spot a house that's left empty a lot of the time. A few simple enquiries tell them who's the owner. Anyone living in that sort of neighbourhood is bound to have valuables. They'd assume that Mister Lambert keeps spare keys in the country and drive down to make a reconnaissance.'

She shook her head doubtfully. 'I find all this beyond me, frankly, Inspector. It just doesn't make sense.'

'It may not to you, miss. I'll admit it's a long shot, but you still might have noticed a stranger hanging round the place. I'd like you to attend an identity parade at Chelsea Police Station – see if you recognize this man.'

'You mean go with you to *London*.'

'It wouldn't take long,' he insisted. 'We can't force you to attend, of course, but your assistance just might prove invaluable.'

'Does Mister Lambert know about this?'

'No, miss, he doesn't. We haven't spoken to him since this morning. But if you'd like to check with him first, do so by all means.'

She thought quickly. She had nothing to lose. She'd just spoken to Mallory and she'd never clapped eyes on Nick Berry. It would seem strange if she refused to co-operate.

'No,' she replied. 'He's been through a very unpleasant experience. I don't want to bother him further.' She glanced down at her clothes. 'Hadn't I better change first?'

'Good Lord, no,' he said smiling broadly. 'You look just fine, miss. And don't worry. If you don't recognize this man, you won't hear from us again, I promise.'

She took her green Barbour jacket from the coatstand and left the hallway lights burning. She sat next to Bellamy in the back of the waiting Rover.

'It's not often I get the chance to meet a lady like you,' he said.

She put a cigarette between her lips and touched flame to it. 'It's not often I get the chance of a ride with a detective-inspector.'

Chapter Three

Mallory left his flat wearing a track suit and sneakers. It was a bleak morning and his sleep had been troubled. There'd been no call from Lucy Ashton since he had last spoken to her. He'd dialled her number repeatedly without obtaining an answer. He jogged up Limerston Street, shoulders squared, his pony-tail bouncing, his cheeks puffed out like a trombone-player.

He slowed as he neared Earls Court. It was a seedy neighbourhood that was a magnet for Australians and New Zealanders working their way round the world. They served beer in pubs, waited on table in restaurants and hung out with the teenage hookers who congregated outside the Underground station. It was a world in which people arrived and left unnoticed, their presence ignored on the electoral rolls or community charge registers. It was the sort of place where Nick Berry felt comfortable.

Mallory stopped in front of a Victorian house showing the same exterior marks of neglect and faded gentility as the rest of the street. Spray drifted in Mallory's direction. He looked over the railings, shielding his face. A woman was hosing the basement steps.

'Excuse me!' he called. 'I'm looking for Nick Berry?'

She lowered the hose, eyeing him with the look of a woman with few illusions.

'Room Two,' she said shortly. 'Press the buzzer.'

Mallory thumbed the button. A voice in the entryphone said, 'Why don't you fuck off?'

'It's me,' said Mallory. 'Open the door!'

He stepped into an untidy hallway noisy with the sound of disparate television channels. There was a smell of bacon frying, a pile of unclaimed post on the metal table.

The door to Number Two opened on Mallory's left. Sunday newspapers were strewn across the floor. There was a sink against the wall, an electric kettle on the counter beside it. The windows were closed. The air stank of hash.

Nick tipped some clothes from the chair, making room for Mallory to sit. He was wearing his shirt and underpants and a day's growth of beard. He pounded the pillows and sprawled on the bed.

'So what's the news? You don't look too happy.'

Mallory turned off the two-bar heater. 'We've got a problem. Lucy left a message on my answering-machine telling me to call her back. So that's what I did. But she had someone there when I finally got hold of her. She promised she'd be in touch with me later last night. I've heard nothing. Added to which, her phone doesn't answer. I'm worried. I think she may have had Lambert with her.'

Nick's face showed no trace of alarm. 'Forget it. If the law sussed me they'd have been banging on the door by now. All I've had is the bleedin' Jehovah's Witnesses. I thought it was them again when you buzzed.'

Mallory's nose thinned. 'It's Lucy I'm concerned about. I've got to know what she's said to Lambert.'

'She ain't in no position to open her mouth,' said Nick. 'Remind her of that when you get hold of her. In the mean time you've got what you wanted.'

Mallory smiled in spite of himself. 'It's weird. I came round here expecting to find you on tenterhooks and here you are telling me not to worry. How are you off for money?'

Nick nodded across at the rickety wardrobe. 'I've still got the last two Social Security cheques. That'll do me for a couple of days.'

'What about your probation officer? Are you making your reports?'

Nick placed a finger on the side of his nose. 'Sweet as a nut. And I meant what I said last night. I'm a reformed character, mate, make no mistake about it.'

'I'm glad to hear it,' said Mallory.

Nick pulled on his trousers. 'Tell you what, let's go out and have a beer.'

'I can't do it,' said Mallory. 'I've got to get back to the flat. There'll probably be a message from Lucy. I'll meet you in the King's Head at half-past eleven tomorrow morning. There's bound to be some news by then. OK?'

Nick waved from the bed. 'Be lucky, mate!'

Mallory let himself out of the house. He was sweating by the time he reached home. He stripped off his clothes and lowered himself into a tub of steaming water. He lay on his back. An idea occurred as he was drying himself. He padded into the sitting-room wrapped in the towel and rang Directory Enquiries.

'Which town, please?' said the operator.

'Corton Bassett in Surrey. I think it comes under Ripley.'

'And the name and address?'

'Anne Ridler. I'm not sure about the address.'

There was a pause; then a recorded voice supplied the information. 'The number you require is 0483 522 611.'

A woman's voice replied. 'This is Martin Mallory,' he said. 'I'm a lecturer at the Wycherly Foundation. I believe you know Lucy Ashton. I've been trying to reach her number since late last night but I can't get an answer. I wonder if you could help me?'

'Sorry,' she said. 'I didn't quite get your name.'

He repeated it. 'She's a friend of mine.'

'We had supper together on Friday night,' she told him, 'and I saw her in the Cash-'n'-Carry on Saturday morning.'

'I talked to her Saturday evening and she promised to

call me back. I wondered if she'd gone away.'

'How well do you know her?'

'I wouldn't say that well,' he answered.

She chuckled. 'That explains it. Lucy's a great one for putting things off. I wouldn't worry too much. She's probably gone out for the day. I'm sure she'll get back to you sooner or later.'

It was almost midnight when he called the cottage again. There was still no reply.

Mallory opened the curtains on another grey day. Frost sparkled on the window panes. He finished his breakfast and glanced at his watch. Ten twenty. Lucy should be in her office by now. He punched out the number and waited.

A woman said, 'Wycherly Foundation.'

'It's Martin Mallory.' His tone was casual. 'Is Lucy there?'

'Just a minute,' the girl said.

It came as a shock to hear Lambert's voice on the line. Mallory hesitated. 'I'm sorry about this, Mister Lambert. The girl's made a mistake. It was Lucy I wanted to speak to.'

'I'm afraid she's not here. Is there anything I can do?'

'She's not sick, I hope?'

'No. She phoned me on Saturday night, saying she felt that she needed a break. I didn't pay too much attention. She's done it before. She gets herself in a state about something or other and takes off for a few days. If it was anyone else I suppose I'd have to do something about it. But what would we do without Lucy? This is part of her make-up. If she feels that she's under pressure, she just gets in her car and comes back a new woman. You're sure there's nothing I can do?'

'Not really,' said Mallory. 'We're changing the syllabus next term. I wondered if Lucy'd remembered to order the new textbooks.'

'I honestly have no idea,' said Lambert. 'Are you at home?'

'Yes,' said Mallory.

'Then I tell you what. I'll be here all day tomorrow. Drop in and tell me about this new syllabus. It's been a long time since we've had a chat.'

'I'll do that,' said Mallory. 'I'm sorry to have troubled you.'

Lambert's manner had been completely natural.

Mallory donned his old scarlet-lined duffle-coat, made sure that the answering-machine was switched on and went down to the street. A man was selling roast chestnuts from a brazier outside the pub on the corner. Discarded shells littered the pavement. People no longer cared about litter. London had become one of Europe's dirtiest capitals. A few early-morning drinkers stood at the long bar on the left, troubled and only too ready to share their experiences. Mallory avoided making eye-contact with them and carried his tonic water to a table near the entrance. Half an hour passed. An hour. There was no sign of Nick. It was after one when Mallory drove north to Cathcart Road. He drew up in front of Nick's lodging-house. The landlady was closing the gate at the top of the basement steps. She was wearing long boots and a ratty fur coat.

Mallory lowered the window. 'Do you know if Mister Berry's at home?'

'Went out early this morning with two men,' she answered indifferently.

'Do you know where he went?' he pressed.

'No idea,' she replied.

He felt his toes stiffen. Apart from himself only two people had Nick's address: the probation officer and Lucy. He knew then that Nick must have been arrested. He drove back to his flat and checked his answering-machine. The tape recorded three separate calls but no message. He sat on the couch and dialled Patrick O'Callaghan's office number. A woman put him through to the lawyer.

Mallory's voice was shaking. 'I've got to see you, Patrick. It's urgent.'

'You'll have to make it quick,' said the lawyer. 'I've got a meeting at three.'

'I'm leaving now,' said Mallory. He put the stolen folder in a shopping-bag, carried it down to his car and drove to O'Callaghan's office.

The Georgian house had been converted to business premises. A brass plate on the second floor read:

PATRICK O'CALLAGHAN
Solicitor & Commissioner for Oaths

A pleasant-faced woman greeted him. 'Good morning, Mister Mallory. Patrick's waiting for you.'

Mallory walked through to the office beyond. The lawyer rose from his desk. He was a delicately boned man with thinning dark hair and a narrow moustache. His black barathea jacket had cuffs on the sleeves. His eccentric appearance disguised a keen brain. People often found his gentle manner misleading. He stretched out his hand over a haphazard pile of papers.

Mallory placed the folder in front of the lawyer. 'This was stolen from a safe in Hollywood Mews last Friday. I'm one of the people responsible.'

The room was suddenly quiet. There was a photograph of O'Callaghan's parents on the wall behind him taken at the Bayreuth Festival, pink-tied briefs on the floor. He spoke into the intercom. 'Don't put any calls through, I'm busy.'

He scanned the two pages of typescript and pushed them back across the desk, frowning.

'What is it?'

'I'm not sure,' Mallory admitted. 'It's going to be hard to explain.'

O'Callaghan sat, tapping his teeth with a small gold

32

pencil. Mallory summoned his courage and spoke without interruption. His confidence had gone by the time he had finished.

O'Callaghan put his pencil down. 'I find this hard to believe. I mean how *could* you get involved in something like this?'

'I loved the girl,' Mallory said stubbornly. 'We were going to get married. Suddenly she was out of my life. I had no idea where she'd gone. Then Lucy Ashton said that Lambert kept a file of the student transfers. She promised to help me get hold of it. That's what you're looking at.'

'Didn't you ask yourself why she'd be doing that, a woman in her position?' said the lawyer.

'I didn't think much about it at first. I mean, I knew she'd had this affair with Lambert, but that was history. If somebody gives you a hand when you're drowning you don't ask for reasons.'

O'Callaghan looked at him steadily. 'You don't seem to realize your position. You're in trouble, Martin. The way I see things, you're facing a charge of receiving stolen property, conspiracy even. What do you think a judge would make of it? Suborning a man on parole to commit burglary, a man you've been visiting in prison, for God's sake?'

Mallory sought to defend himself. 'But it wasn't *like* that. We were friends. I told him about my predicament. He offered to help me.'

'A convicted felon?' O'Callaghan intoned. 'That only makes matters worse. You're the instigator, Martin. Without you none of this would have happened.'

Mallory lifted his head. 'So what do you think I should do?'

'There's only one thing you *can* do,' said O'Callaghan. 'Make a clean breast of things. I'll get hold of the officer in charge and we'll see him together.'

'I can't do that,' Mallory said flatly. 'I can't face the shame and disgrace. I'd sooner put a hole in my head.

What happens if I send the papers back to Lambert?'

O'Callaghan clicked his tongue. 'And if he finds out the truth?'

'There's something I haven't told you,' said Mallory. 'I was supposed to meet Nick but he didn't turn up. His landlady said he left with two men early this morning. I think he's been arrested. That's why I came here.'

'You can't be sure of that,' said the lawyer.

'I don't have to be sure. I spoke to Lambert a couple of hours ago. He said that Lucy called in saying she was feeling under a lot of pressure and needed some time off. He didn't sound too concerned but I'm worried, Patrick. First Lucy, now Nick.'

'That's what a guilty conscience does,' said O'Callaghan. 'Your best bet is to take my advice. Get in first.'

Mallory picked up the bag with the file and collected his duffle-coat. 'I seem to have been wasting my time,' he said bitterly.

O'Callaghan held up both hands. 'OK. I've given my advice as a lawyer. You don't want to take it. But you're my friend and I can't let you go away thinking I've let you down. I know one man who just might be able to help.'

'Who is it?' asked Mallory.

'An ex-policeman, but don't let that put you off. He resigned as a matter of principle. He's got a strong aversion to conventional ideas about right and wrong. He's a strange man in many ways but he's one hundred per cent reliable. Anything you say to him will be kept in total confidence. I don't know if he'll see you but it's certainly worth a try. Would you like me to call him?'

Mallory sank back on the chair, his hope rekindled. 'Anything, please!'

O'Callaghan lifted the phone. 'John? It's Patrick. Look, I've got a friend here with a very big problem. It's the sort of thing you might well be interested in. Can I send him along to see you? I'll tell you the story later.'

He put the phone down and scribbled an address on a piece of paper. 'Be on his boat at four o'clock. His name is John Raven. He won't expect to be paid for his help if he decides to give it, but he's a friend not a charitable organization, so keep that in mind.'

Mallory nodded. 'I'll let you know how it goes.'

Chapter Four

The mooring-chains groaned and creaked as the *Albatross* wallowed in the wake of a passing police-launch. John Raven was lying flat on his back, his left leg raised on a pillow. It was two months since his varicose vein had been excised but its ghost still gave him twinges of pain. He was forty-eight years old, six feet three inches tall with wide bony shoulders, arctic-blue eyes and greying fair hair that needed trimming. He had on Wrangler jeans, a black turtle-neck sweater and a pair of Reeboks.

The *Albatross* had been his home for the last fifteen years, a converted brewers' barge that had once been used to haul barley. It was the first real home he had ever had. He had been seven years old when his parents were killed in a car crash. A maiden aunt brought him up in her home in Suffolk. She had put his name down for Harrow, hoping that he would follow his father into the Civil Service. His aunt died during his last year at school, leaving him £360,000 in trust until he was twenty-one. A year after his majority, he joined the Metropolitan Police Force. He passed out of Hendon, equal top of class with a Hong Kong-born Chinese named Jerry Soo. Raven's first posting was an East End district where crime was indigenous. His promotion was rapid over the next few years. At thirty-three he was a detective-inspector on the Flying Squad. Aware that colleagues were on the take from a drug-dealing syndicate, Raven informed his superiors.

A week later he found himself in front of a Disciplinary Board charged with making unfounded allegations against fellow-officers. Jerry Soo had been in Taiwan on vacation. Raven took his problem to a man he had been at school with. Patrick O'Callaghan had listened sympathetically. Raven complained that he'd taken an oath to uphold law and order yet he couldn't get justice himself. O'Callaghan did his best to dissuade Raven from taking hasty action but Raven was adamant. He resigned from the Force, renouncing all rights to pension and benefits.

Daylight was beginning to dwindle beyond the panoramic sweep of the double-glazed windows. Raven activated the electric motor, shuttling the heavy blue velvet curtains the length and breadth of the sitting-room. His eyes lit on his wife's photograph on top of the French writing-bureau. Kirstie Raven was a Canadian fashion-photographer presently on a shoot in Goa. She'd been away for three weeks and he missed her sorely.

Apart from Raven's cherished Paul Klee painting, there was little of any great worth on the boat. The much-darned Aubusson, the writing-bureau and the silver had come from his aunt's home in Suffolk. Kirstie and he had bought the remainder together. A firm of Medway shipfitters had done the conversion, putting a deck over the hold and adding a red-cedarwood superstructure. There were two bedrooms, with the bathroom between at the end of the short corridor, a large well-equipped kitchen with a Welsh oak dresser. The sitting-room occupied the rest of the space, the windows following the rounded curve of the stern. The Paul Klee hung under a picture-light near the door to the deck. White-painted shelves with storage cupboards underneath supported a Bang & Olufsen music centre. A black-lacquered cabinet held the drinks and the two couches were upholstered in blue velvet matching the curtains.

The buzzer sounded at the foot of the steps leading down from the Embankment. The gangway served the

Albatross and the rusting old MTB that belonged to Raven's Californian neighbour who sold Oriental bric-à-brac from a store in the alley-way opposite.

Raven pressed the release-button, turned on the deck-light and stood in the doorway. A man in a duffle-coat with a scarf round his neck appeared, carrying a plastic shopping-bag. His lank hair was pulled back in a pony-tail.

'I'm Martin Mallory,' he said.

'Come in,' Raven invited. He waved a hand at the sofa. 'Make yourself comfortable. Would you like coffee or something stronger?'

'Coffee's fine,' said Mallory. He put the shopping-bag down on the sofa and took off his coat, revealing a tweed jacket with elbow-patches, grey flannel trousers and a pair of chukka boots.

Raven took a jar of Salvadorean instant coffee from the kitchen dresser and made a brew that would have fuelled a jet engine. He put the mug on the rectangular table in front of his guest and lowered himself into his favourite chair. 'I've had a long talk with Patrick, so I know your problems. He's a very good lawyer. Why don't you want to take his advice?'

Mallory took a sip from the mug and shuddered. 'I just couldn't face it. I don't have that sort of courage.'

Raven inspected him dispassionately. 'So what makes you think that I can help you?'

Mallory offered a wan smile. 'Hope, I suppose. It all seems like some horrible nightmare.'

It was a phrase that Raven had heard many times before. A refusal to face the facts. He lifted the lid of the chased silver box and removed a Gitane. His attempt at blowing a smoke-ring failed as usual.

'I'm not running an agony column, if that's what you're looking for. God alone knows I've made a lot of mistakes myself in the past. But I've always had some sort of idea what I was doing. You don't seem to have had any thought of the consequences.'

Mallory's face flushed. 'I was in love. It's as simple as that.'

Raven settled back in his chair. 'How long have you been working at the Wycherly Foundation?'

'Four years.'

'And how old are you?'

'I'm thirty-four,' replied Mallory.

'And your girlfriend?'

'Twenty-two.'

Raven flicked his cigarette at the ashtray. 'How many pupils have been transferred during your time?'

Mallory's shoulders rose and fell. 'Three. I'd get a note from the Bursar's Office. I never asked questions. It was none of my business in any case. But Li was different. I wanted to marry her, you see. It just seemed impossible that she'd leave without telling me why.'

'Have you contacted her home?'

'You mean in Kowloon? I didn't even know where she lived. She was a very private person and never talked about her family. I asked some of the other students but they couldn't help. The Bursar referred me to Lambert but I couldn't go to him for obvious reasons. That's when Lucy Ashton came into the picture.' He took the manila folder from the shopping-bag and gave it to Raven. 'That's what Nick Berry found in the safe.'

Raven scanned the closely typed sheets and frowned. 'What the hell is it?' he asked, putting the folder down on the glass-topped table.

Mallory moved his head despairingly. 'I was hoping that Lucy would tell me. Now she's suddenly vanished.'

'Let's get back to your girlfriend,' said Raven. 'We're talking about a woman half your age from an entirely different culture and background. Didn't it occur to you that she might have felt that this affair was getting out of hand? That this was the best way of ending it?'

Mallory's mouth set stubbornly. 'I'm prepared to accept that she's out of my life, if that's what you mean. It's what's happened since that frightens me.'

'OK, let's try to deal with that,' said Raven. 'According to Patrick you think that Nick's been arrested. Is that right?'

'Put yourself in my place,' said Mallory. 'Lambert's cleaner got a clear look at Nick, that's number one. Number two is we arranged to meet this morning. He never turned up. His landlady said he left the house early this morning with two men. What would you think?'

Raven drew on his cigarette. 'What about Lucy?'

Mallory looked glum. 'Not a word. I invented an excuse to call Lambert. He just said that she'd gone off for a few days on a leave of absence.'

'But you don't believe him?' Raven queried. 'Is that what you're saying?'

'I think he's hiding something,' Mallory said stoutly.

Raven extinguished his cigarette and lifted the telephone.

A man's voice said, 'Detective-Inspector Soo speaking.'

'I'm at home,' said Raven. 'Can you talk?'

'It'll have to be quick,' answered Soo. 'I've got a desk full of work and I've got to leave early. I'm taking Louise to a concert.' Soo's wife was a Taiwanese who played cello with the Purcell String Orchestra.

'It'll only take a few minutes,' urged Raven. 'I want to know if you people are holding someone called Nicholas Berry. He could have been nicked this morning. Can you do that for me?'

'I'll call you back in five,' promised Soo.

The two men waited in silence until the telephone came to life again.

'I've got his CRO sheet on the screen in front of me. Nicholas George Berry, born Camberwell, April fourth, nineteen sixty-two. He's got a couple of previous. It says here he left the Scrubs on parole ten days ago. There's no record of the Met having him in custody. Is that any good to you?'

'Thanks,' said Raven. 'Give my love to Louise and enjoy your concert.'

He turned to Mallory. 'The police haven't got him. He probably found something better to do.'

The news seemed to disturb Mallory even more. 'I'm at my wits' end,' he said.

Raven thought for a minute. There was no doubt in his mind that Mallory was gripped fast in self-delusion. But the question of Lucy's disappearance merited some real consideration. An idea shaped in Raven's brain.

He pushed the telephone across the table. 'I want you to call Lambert,' he said. 'Tell him that a friend just died in a car crash. Don't go into details. Just say you're having to take care of the funeral arrangements and you'll need a few days off.'

Mallory stared down at the receiver. 'He's not a fool. He's bound to be suspicious.'

'Do it!' Raven said forcefully.

Mallory's lips moved as he composed the number. He spoke for a few brief minutes before replacing the handset. 'I don't get it. All he said was to take as long as I needed. If the worst came to the worst he'd get a supply teacher in from the agency.'

'Did he mention Lucy?'

'Not a word,' replied Mallory. 'But he's already told me what happened. There's nothing more he could say, I suppose.'

'Has she ever done this before? I mean, taking off without warning?'

'I wouldn't know,' Mallory answered. 'We were never that close. Lambert says that it's something she does when she feels under pressure. If it was anyone else he'd have sacked her.'

Raven walked across to the window and back. 'Tell me about her neighbours. Is there anyone who could give us some information?'

'I doubt it,' said Mallory. 'The Bursar and his wife live next door but they wouldn't know any more than Lambert. There's a farm a couple of hundred yards away and a pub at the end of the lane and that's it.' He dabbed at an eye with a handkerchief. 'I'm not very good at this kind of thing.'

Raven studied the other man's face. 'Don't you ever think about anyone else but yourself?' he challenged.

'Like who?' Mallory demanded. 'It's time someone thought about me instead of leaving me holding the can.'

Mallory's defiance hardened Raven's impatience. 'I've come across a lot of people like you,' he said. 'People who think they've got some God-given right to be bailed out of trouble. If you want my help you're going to have to do what I tell you. I want you to go home and start acting like a man for a change.' He pointed down at the folder. 'I'll take care of this for the moment.'

Mallory donned his coat and scarf. 'You've just taken a weight off my shoulders.'

Raven opened the door. 'Don't fool yourself. The weight's only shifted. Don't go out, I'll talk to you later tonight.'

He waited until Mallory disappeared and closed the sitting-room door. It was a quarter to six. O'Callaghan was still in his office.

'He just left,' said Raven. 'I'll give you my impression for what it's worth. He's one of those bleeding hearts who'll dance for anyone who can whistle salvation. But I don't think he's lying.'

'Are you going to help him or not? Just give me a plain answer. I don't want to know the details.'

'I wouldn't dream of offending your high moral standards,' said Raven. 'But the answer to your question is that I'm thinking about it.'

Raven went through to the guest room. One of the beds had been stored in the hold, making space for a small draughtsman's table with a hundred-watt inspection-lamp poised above a personal word processor. A fax machine stood against the wall. Shelves carried a comprehensive array of reference books and a pile of Ordnance Survey maps. Raven unlocked a cupboard and took out a briefcase containing his out-of-date Metropolitan Police warrant-card and a picture of him standing next to Jerry Soo at the Hendon College passing-out ceremony. Jerry had been abandoned as an infant, left on the steps of the Methodist Memorial Hospital and adopted by three Scottish nurses. At the age of twelve he spoke Mandarin, the Hong Kong dialect and English, all without accent. His friendship with Raven endured through the years. Each had served as the other's best man. They went on holidays together, fishing for salmon, riding in the Alentejo. Soo remained one of the few people Raven trusted implicitly.

He slipped the manila folder on the shelf and rummaged below until he found a flat tin box the size of a pocket book. It held an assortment of handmade burglary tools inside, the steel dulled with a film of petroleum jelly. The skeleton keys were arranged according to type and size. There were pass keys to most commercial locks, a variety of picks and a pair of dental forceps. The package had arrived through the post many years before, a wry parting gift from an old adversary who had seen the light and emigrated to New Zealand.

The box fitted snugly in the pocket of Raven's Burberry. He made sure that the answering-machine was functioning and locked the door to the deck behind him.

The dark-blue Orion in the cul-de-sac was a new acquisition with a five-speed gearbox and plenty of leg-room behind the steering-wheel. Raven put the map on the dashboard and slotted his seat-belt. Once on the Portsmouth road, he kept to the middle lane. Each vehicle was a time capsule, its occupants engrossed in their own affairs. Raven turned off at the exit to Corton Bassett. Sodium vapour lamps lit the ramp leading down to the trading estate. Milk trucks were loading for the early-morning run to London. Raven followed the sign to Ripley as far as a filling-station. A pub on the corner opposite advertised Hot Food and Real Ale. A few cars were parked outside the curtained windows. Raven swung right into the lane, checked the map again and drove slowly forward behind dimmed headlamps. Thick hedges gave way to post-and-rail fencing. A barn loomed ahead, a pond and a farmhouse. Then a bend in the lane revealed two thatched cottages standing side by side. Raven backed the car into the open barn and cut the engine and head-lamps. He took a torch from the glove compartment and walked forward cautiously. Lights shone on both floors of the Bursar's cottage; Lucy's car port was empty. He fol-lowed the wall to the rear of her cottage and stood with his ears on stalks. Rhododendron bushes shielded him from the windows next door. He craned down and shone the torch on Lucy's back door. The tip of the key pro-truded. He tried the handle. The door had been locked from inside. He took the dental forceps from the box in his pocket and clamped them on the end of the key. He turned his wrist full-circle and the door swung open. He closed it gently. The torch picked out an oil-fired Aga stove and a bag of groceries on the table.

He tiptoed into the hallway. The door to the room in front of him was ajar. A firescreen was propped in front of dead ashes in a basket. He followed the narrow beam of light up the stairs.

The two doors on the second floor were ajar. The one on the left was the bathroom. Raven moved into the bedroom next door. He made sure that the curtains were properly closed and placed his ear on the outer wall. The voices from the Bursar's cottage were barely audible. He glanced round the room. A pair of flannel pyjamas lay folded at the foot of the neatly made bed. A bottle of Perrier water and a glass stood near the bed. He peeped inside the wardrobe and saw rows of clothes suspended on nylon hangers, boots and shoes cleaned ready for wear. He crossed the Afghan rug to the dressing-table and opened the top right-hand drawer. A cardboard box inside contained a birth certificate in the name of Lucy Helen Ashton, born in Salisbury 3/6/59. Next came a British passport bearing the same name and particulars. There was a cheque book and four credit cards. He pushed the box back and closed the drawer. He shone the torch into the bathroom and saw a bowl filled with liquid on the ledge beneath the mirror. He detected the shape of two contact lenses and straightened his back, thinking of a woman getting ready to leave for a few days' rest. There was no sign of hurried departure. And why had she left her contact lenses behind? It was a matter of need, not vanity.

He went down the stairs to the sitting-room. There was nothing there that gave him a clue. The television set was turned off, a copy of Saturday's *Times* on the sofa. He stiffened as headlamps swept across the curtained windows. He was in the kitchen when he heard the front door being opened. The stairs creaked under a man's firm tread. A light came on in the bedroom as Raven slipped out through the kitchen door. There was no time to lock it again. A Bentley Continental was parked in the car port outside. Raven jogged back to the barn. The lights were still on in the cottage when he drove out of the lane.

Raven left the Ford Orion at the bottom of Park Walk and walked back to Elm Park Mansions. Mallory answered the door-buzzer. It was a long climb to the top floor. Mallory hurried him into the sitting-room. It was more or less what Raven had expected to find. He took off his Burberry and lowered himself on to the small couch in front of the silent television. Mallory fetched a chair from the bedroom.

'Did you know that Lucy wore contact lenses?' said Raven.

Mallory seemed surprised by the question. 'Of course. She's short-sighted.'

'Has she got any spares?'

Mallory lifted his shoulders. 'I wouldn't think so. She

only started wearing them a couple of months ago. She was trying them out. She wanted to know which kind suited her best, the hard or the soft.'

'I just left her cottage,' said Raven. 'There was a pair of contact lenses in the bathroom. I looked in her dressing-table. She's left her passport and cheque book behind and her credit cards. And I'll tell you something else. There's a bag of groceries on the kitchen table, butter and stuff. And the Aga's still lit.'

Mallory's face lost its colour. 'She was all right on Saturday night. I spoke to her.'

'But you haven't heard since?'

'No,' said Mallory. 'I've been sitting here expecting her to call.'

'Does Lambert have a key to the cottage?'

'He's got keys to both of them.'

'And he drives a dark-blue Bentley?'

'Yes.'

'I was lucky,' said Raven. 'I went out the back door as he came in the front.' He lit a cigarette, keeping his eyes on Mallory's crumpling face. 'I don't know what's happened to her any more than you do, but I'm pretty sure she didn't leave voluntarily. And if I'm right, that doesn't improve your situation. I think you ought to start thinking hard about Patrick's advice.'

Mallory's voice squeaked out of register. 'You mean go to the police! You know I can't do that! You promised to help me, for God's sake. I'm *relying* on you!'

Raven had no particular regard for the man, but he was a friend of Patrick's. And that counted. 'Then we'll just have to play it by ear,' he said, donning his raincoat. 'There's nothing more we can do tonight. I'll call you again in the morning. It's possible you may have heard something from Lucy by then.'

He reversed the Orion into the cul-de-sac and killed the headlamps. Kirstie was due to phone any moment. Goa was four and a half hours ahead of the UK. It was difficult to get a line during the day. The sound of music grew louder as he descended the steps to the landing-stage. Hank Lauterbach was entertaining. Riding-lights illuminated the network of ropes, rafts and gangways linking the flotilla of houseboats.

He let himself on to the *Albatross*. He put the burglary tools back in their hiding-place, made himself a pastrami sandwich and drank a bottle of Labatt lager in front of the sitting-room TV, watching the ten o'clock news.

The phone rang beside him. He zapped the set off and grabbed the receiver. 'Kirstie? How are you, darling?'

Her voice came in sound waves. 'Just fine. Listen, it's starting to blow here. They're expecting an early monsoon. I'm flying home via New York.'

'And abandon the shoot?'

'No, no,' she said quickly. 'We're just having to work faster. This new model's a honey. She photographs brilliantly and what's more she can get up in the morning.'

'Why aren't you coming home direct?'

'The Art Director's got an April deadline and there's a lot of retouching for me to do. So I'm using their studio. I should be back by the thirtieth.'

'Great,' he replied. 'You've been gone too long. I'm getting tired of sleeping alone.'

Her voice was prim. 'Self-restraint strengthens the character. Is Mrs Burrows taking proper care of you?'

The cleaning lady had been with him since his bachelor days. Her resentment of Kirstie's arrival had waned to a guarded neutrality. She continued to regard Raven as her personal property.

'She's in good form,' he said. 'Why don't you send her a card? She'd like that.'

Kirstie sniffed. 'I doubt it. Look, this is a terrible line and it's almost three in the morning. I'll be at the Carlyle in New York. I'll call you from there.'

She blew a kiss into the mouthpiece and broke the connection, leaving him with a feeling of loss. He knew as surely as his heartbeat how much she loved him and the knowledge shamed him. One of these days, one of these mornings, he'd wake up a changed man, purged of whatever it was that drove him to do the things that she feared and hated.

He turned off the sitting-room lights and got into bed.

Chapter Five

It was a quarter to ten the following morning, a grey overcast day with a sense of ominous stillness. Raven turned away from the sitting-room window. He had been up for two hours, prowling restlessly in an effort to rid his mind of uncertainty. He was wearing his grey herringbone tweed suit and a sober tie. The circumstances warranted an appearance of respectability.

He took the phone in his lap and dialled. Mallory's voice answered cautiously. 'Yes?'

'Have you heard anything?' asked Raven.

Mallory spoke like a man with one foot in the door getting ready to bolt.

'Nothing. Not a bloody word from either of them. Somebody called just after midnight but the phone was dead by the time I got to it. I mean, I'm sitting here worried stiff and they don't even bother to get in touch!'

'Forget it,' said Raven impatiently. 'We've got other things to think about. I want to know where Nick Berry lives.'

'Nick?' Mallory repeated. 'Why do you want to know? I told you yesterday, he isn't there.'

Raven's jaw muscles hardened. 'Just give me the address.'

Mallory supplied the information reluctantly. 'It's Cathcart Road, the second house on the left coming from Finborough Road. Room Two.'

'Has he got his own bell or what?'

'There's an entryphone. I don't want him to know I've been talking to someone else about this business.'

'It doesn't matter what he thinks,' said Raven. 'How do I get hold of the landlady?'

'She lives in the basement,' said Mallory. 'But for God's sake be careful. She's already seen my car.'

'I told you before,' warned Raven, 'you got yourself into this mess. Nobody twisted your arm, remember.'

Mallory's voice was chastened. 'I know. But you've got to understand my position.'

'Oh, but I do,' Raven said grimly. 'And I don't much like what I see. You're going to have to start pulling your weight, my friend, or find another shoulder to cry on. Do you hear what I'm saying?'

'I'm sorry,' Mallory answered abjectly.

Raven put the phone down as the door slammed at the end of the gangway. Mrs Burrows came into the room. She was a short thin woman dressed in several layers of clothing. She loosened her coat, looking Raven up and down with dark button eyes.

'We don't see you in a suit very often. What happened? Did somebody die?'

'Business,' he answered. Her mind ran on death, doom and disaster. If she knew of none, she invented her own. She had been with him for twelve years, long before his marriage, and viewed Kirstie as a challenger to her own privileged position. There were constant references to Raven's life as a carefree bachelor. She had viewed his retirement from the Police Force as a grave error of judgement brought about by Kirstie's influence. Kirstie had handled the situation with a determined display of unfailing civility, refusing to take offence at Mrs Burrows' proprietorial posture, content to make it clear that her forbearance was limited. Over the years, the relationship between the two women had become what Raven thought of as a kind of armed truce. Mrs Burrows continued to snipe occasionally while Kirstie remained untouched.

Mrs Burrows hung her coat in the corridor closet and helped Raven on with his Burberry.

He shrugged into the sleeves. 'I spoke to Mrs Raven last night. We're going to have her back sooner than we expected.'

She made a purse of her lips. 'And not before time, if you'll pardon me saying so. It was different in my day. We knew our responsibilities then. A man shouldn't be left on his own, you know.'

It was the stern voice of another world that spoke. 'She sent her regards,' said Raven.

Mrs Burrows lifted her head and drew in her scrawny chest. 'It just isn't good enough. We might have been poor but we knew our duty.'

Raven withdrew from the contest. Whenever he was alone on the boat, Mrs Burrows insisted on preparing stodgy meals for him, oblivious of the fact that these were dropped overboard for the fish and the gulls to consume. It was a small price to pay for her peace of mind. Things wouldn't be the same without her.

'Don't worry about food for tonight,' he said. 'I'm having supper with a friend.'

The information did nothing to mellow her mood. 'I hope it isn't that Maggie Sanchez,' she said darkly. 'That's another one who spells trouble. She drinks too much if you want my opinion.'

'Nobody does,' he said firmly. 'Maggie's a very old friend of mine and a very sad lady. Try to be a little more charitable.'

She put her head on one side and peered up at him. 'Is that who it is you're seeing?'

'No, it isn't,' he said. He put his hands on her shoulders and pointed her into the kitchen. 'Bye-bye, Mrs Burrows.'

He made his way up the steps to the Embankment and smelled the first acrid hint of fog drifting up from the river. The nine o'clock news had foretold it. He drove the Orion north and stopped a few yards along Cathcart Road.

This was the heart of bedsitter land, the home of the dispossessed. The exteriors of the houses showed a uniform state of neglect. He climbed the few steps and tried the entryphone. There was no response. He took a look through the flap on the letter-box. A strip of cloth on the inside impeded his vision. He straightened his back and descended the steps to the basement.

A length of garden hose was coiled on a stand under a curtained window. A woman of forty wearing slacks thrust into high boots and a scarf around her head stood in the doorway. She looked at him with the assessing stare of someone who retained few illusions in life.

'Yes?' she said.

He greeted her courteously. 'Good morning, madam. I apologize for disturbing you but I'm trying to get hold of Mister Berry. His entryphone doesn't answer.'

'Well, you won't find him here,' she retorted. 'He went out early this morning.' A black tom-cat with battle-scarred ears wreathed through her legs and trod delicately over the wet flagstones.

'Do you happen to know where he's gone?' asked Raven.

She glanced up at the street. 'Are you from the police?'

'Good Lord, no,' said Raven. He showed her his driving-licence. Drawing deep on his charm, he asked, 'May I speak to you in confidence?'

Her eyes flickered momentarily. 'That depends. He's only been here a couple of weeks. I don't know anything about him.'

She pulled a pack of cigarettes from her trouser pocket. Raven gave her a light. 'It's a delicate matter,' he explained. 'Mister Berry was supposed to be bringing me a letter from my wife this morning but he never showed up. The point is she's expecting an answer. She's not a rational person. If she doesn't get a reply today, she can cause me a lot of trouble. You see the position I'm in.'

She blew a stream of smoke from her nostrils. 'Is Mister Berry a friend of hers?'

'An acquaintance,' said Raven. 'He's just doing me a favour.'

The landlady shrugged. 'Well, why don't you tell her what happened?'

'I don't even know where she is until I get the letter.'

'I'm afraid I can't help you,' she said.

'He might have left the letter in his room,' he pleaded. 'You could come with me. You'd be doing me a very big favour.'

'Nobody ever got rich on doing favours,' she said suggestively.

He opened his wallet and gave her a twenty-pound note. She took a bunch of keys from the table behind her. He followed her up the steps to the hallway above. She opened the door on the left and sat on a chair by the table outside, still smoking her cigarette.

'Don't be too long,' she said.

The grimed windows were hung with dingy curtains and the oxygen-starved air smelled of stale take-away meals. The brown carpet was mapped with stains. The bed was unmade. He took a look inside the flimsy wardrobe. A blue suit with a drip-dry shirt draped over its shoulders hung on a wire coat-hanger. There was a pair of rubber-soled shoes lying on top of a cheap suitcase, an envelope on the shelf above. He glanced out at the hallway. The landlady was scanning the post on the table. The envelope contained two Social Security giro cheques. Each was for thirty-seven pounds fifty pence. He put the giros back in the envelope and left the room.

'No luck,' he told her. 'I'll just have to wait until he turns up, I suppose. But thanks for your help.'

'Anything for a gentleman,' she said, smiling coyly. 'It's too bad about your wife. But I'm usually in of an evening if you're interested.'

'I'll remember that,' he said.

She was back in the basement before he reached the car. He stopped at the first pay phone he saw and dialled

Mallory's number. 'Has Nick got any money?'

'Not as far as I know,' said Mallory. 'I offered him some but he wouldn't take it.'

'The landlady let me look in his room,' said Raven. 'He's got two DHSS giros in the wardrobe. Why hasn't he cashed them?'

'He could have borrowed some money,' Mallory suggested.

'Use your head, for God's sake,' said Raven. 'He's a cheap, scheming villain hoping to make a quick score with these people he left with this morning. It's obvious. He's going to tell them about the robbery. Do you see what I'm getting at?'

'Jesus!' Mallory said feelingly. 'You mean they'd threaten me?'

Raven brought his face close to the mouthpiece, making each word tell. 'I want you out of that flat *now*, Martin! Throw some things in a bag and get out of there fast. Leave your car where it is and wait for me in the Peter Jones cafeteria. Is that clear?'

He put the phone down and fed another coin into the slot. A man answered, 'Danforth Service Apartments, Paul Sinnott speaking.'

'It's John Raven,' he said. 'Have you got a room free?'

'How long do you want it for?'

'We're not sure yet,' said Raven. 'It's for a friend who's having a problem with his wife.'

Sinnott clicked his tongue. 'I don't want any trouble here. I'm running a respectable establishment.'

'There won't *be* any trouble,' said Raven. 'The man's an academic looking for peace and quiet. That's why I thought of you in the first place. Are there phones in the rooms?'

'Of course. The rent doesn't include electricity so everything's metered, including the phone. It goes on the bill. Which floor do you want?'

'Have you got anything downstairs?'

'I've one on the ground floor,' said Sinnott. 'It's at the

front but the windows are double glazed so you don't hear any noise from the street.'

'How much is it?' asked Raven.

'Well,' drawled Sinnott, 'I'll be frank with you. Business is not what you'd call flourishing and the man's a friend of yours. There's a minimum let of a month. I can let him have it for six hundred plus the electricity bill. What's his name?'

'He doesn't want to use it for obvious reasons,' said Raven. 'I'll guarantee the rent. I'll bring him round in half an hour or so.'

He left his car in Cadogan Street and walked a couple of hundred yards to the department store. The cafeteria on the top floor was crowded with women eating lunch. He took his place in the queue at the self-service counter, scanning the large room. He located Mallory sitting alone at a table, staring across Sloane Square. There was a bag on the floor beside him. He turned nervously as Raven dragged the spare chair back. Raven put his coffee-cup down and made space for his elbows. 'Did anyone see you leave the flat?'

Mallory seemed to have difficulty speaking. 'Nobody. I still think you're wrong, you know.'

'I'll do the thinking,' said Raven. 'Elm Park Mansions isn't a good place for you to be at the moment. Too many odd things are happening. And I wouldn't pin your faith on Nick Berry. You're a dead loss as far as he's concerned.' He extended a hand. 'You'd better give me the keys to your flat.'

Mallory reached in his pocket. Raven continued. 'I've booked you into a room in the Danforth Apartments on Hans Crescent. I know the man who runs the place. I've told him you're having wife trouble and you want to stay out of the way for a while. So he won't ask questions.'

A shadow passed across Mallory's face. 'I still think you're wrong about Nick. The trouble is you don't know him.'

'I don't need to,' said Raven. 'I know his kind. That's

enough. Come on, we'd better get moving.'

Mallory put on his duffle-coat and picked up his bag. It was a short walk up Pavilion Road then left on to Basil Street. The Danforth Service Apartments were on the corner opposite a Harrods display-window. The plate-glass entrance opened into a grey-carpeted lobby where an eighteenth-century-style sedan chair added a touch of elegance. Raven pressed the bell marked VISITORS. The entrance-door clicked open and a man emerged from the narrow lift, wearing a light-grey suit.

Raven made the introductions.

Sinnott nodded politely at Mallory. 'I'll show you the room.'

He flicked a switch on the wall. Exterior shutters rolled up on each window, revealing a large double bed covered with a silk spread. There was a telephone on the table beside it. The cream-coloured walls were hung with Toulouse-Lautrec prints. There was a television set with a video recorder on a stand facing the foot of the bed. Raven peeked into the bathroom. There was a plate-glass shower-stall, and towels on the heated rails. Raven pushed the door shut. It was a far cry from the squalor of Nick Berry's lodgings. Mallory was standing glum-faced, watching Raven uncertainly.

Raven swung round on Sinnott. 'What about cooking facilities?'

Sinnott's nose thinned. 'The maid serves a continental breakfast between eight and ten. And there are plenty of places to eat in the neighbourhood. The rooms are cleaned every day by arrangement with tenants. There are only four other people staying at the moment, a Brazilian family, and they're out most of the day so the house is quiet.'

'We'll take it,' said Raven. He wrote a cheque for a month's rent and gave it to Sinnott who put two keys on the bedside table.

'I'm on the top floor if your friend has any problems,'

he said. 'Enjoy your stay with us, sir.' The door to the hallway closed gently behind him.

Raven moved to the window. The Underground station was fifty yards away, angling the junction with Brompton Road.

'You've got everything you want in Harrods,' he told Mallory. 'Restaurants, a bank, a video library. You can have your hair cut and get rid of that coat. And most important of all, you'll be safe.'

Mallory sat on the end of the bed, surly-faced and resentful. 'I'd have felt a lot safer at home. I wasn't expecting anything like this when I went to see Patrick.'

The ingratitude stung like a hornet. 'What *did* you expect?' Raven demanded. 'A bloody medal?'

Mallory's pudgy cheeks reddened. 'There's no need to be so offensive. I'm doing the best I can.'

Raven made no attempt to hide his disdain. 'Then stop whingeing,' he said. 'We don't have to like one another. But as long as you want my support try to act like a man.'

Mallory let his breath go. 'You don't seem to understand what I'm going through.'

'I'm trying,' said Raven. 'Is it the girl that's worrying you?'

'No,' said Mallory. 'It's something else.'

Raven was lost for words for a second. '*Something else!*' he repeated. 'You're the one who doesn't understand. You could be on the verge of total disaster and you sit there bellyaching like a pregnant schoolgirl. What's more important than protecting yourself?'

Mallory raised his head. 'That's what I'm thinking about. I've never laid claim to being a hero. The mere idea of physical violence appals me. It's not part of my nature, for God's sake. I'm not even sure that I'm doing the right thing,' he finished miserably.

'Then you'd better get your priorities in perspective,' Raven said quietly, striding across to the bedside table. He lifted the telephone. The dialling tone purred reassuringly. He put the receiver down. 'Let's get this clear,' he said. 'Nobody can turn the clock back. I'm here because of Patrick. You want me out of it, fine. All you've got to do is say so.'

Mallory gulped despairingly. 'No! I've got to have someone to help me.'

Raven made a note of the phone number. 'I'm willing to do whatever I can. But you've got to help yourself. Otherwise I'm wasting my time. Don't you see that?'

Mallory gave a nod of understanding and threw a hand at the windows. 'What do you want me to do, for God's sake? Sit here like a bloody prisoner?'

'You're letting your imagination run away with you,' said Raven. 'You're free to come and go as you please. Just keep a low profile and stay away from your flat.' Raven smiled. 'We'll work this thing out as long as you do what I tell you. Remember, I'm on your side. I've got the phone number here and I'll keep an eye on your flat. OK?'

The fog outside was lowering like a pall on the city, creeping into doorways and dwellings. Raven travelled home on dipped headlamps and backed into the cul-de-sac. His neighbour's gift shop was still shut, his Harley-Davidson cowled on its stand near the wall. Lauterbach drove a hard bargain with himself. Suffering was part of his enjoyment.

Mrs Burrows had left the lights burning. Raven changed into corduroy slacks, a sweatshirt and lumber-jacket. He needed to think. Physical movement always sparked his imagination. He went out on deck. It was difficult to see the other side of the river. The lamp standards looked like fishbowls suspended in watery vapour. According to Kirstie there were no such things as seasons in England, just weather. He walked north on Oakley Street. Pedestrians hurried by with averted heads as though unwilling to meet what might emerge from the thickening fog.

Raven's thoughts lay with the man he had just left. Mallory was completely out of his depth, floundering and fearful. Raven felt he should have been gentler with him.

The line of traffic moved slowly along the King's Road, the pace set by the lumbering buses. Raven had a solitary meal in a satay restaurant on the Fulham Road and bought a ticket to the cinema on the corner of Drayton Gardens. He left halfway through the programme, bored and for some undefinable reason depressed. He reached the boat shortly after ten o'clock. The sitting-room was warm and welcoming. He undressed and crawled into bed, choosing the side where Kirstie usually slept. Her perfume rose from the pillow where his head lay, a reminder of how empty his life was without the flash of her smile and teasing offbeat humour. He remembered the way she looked at him with star-sapphire eyes, refusing to surrender her point of view. She was loyal, courageous and totally desirable. And best of all she was on her way home.

The phone shrilled, invading Raven's repose. He squirrelled under the duvet and grabbed the receiver. 'Yes?'

Jerry Soo's tone was unusually brusque. 'Where the hell were you last night?'

'I was out,' Raven answered, still half-asleep.

'Don't you check your answering-machine? I left a message.'

'I must have forgotten,' Raven said tetchily. 'What's your problem?'

'It's the guy you asked me about the other day, Nick Berry? The River Police found him drowned just below Hungerford Footbridge.'

'When?'

'Yesterday afternoon. My secretary saw the report and told me. I called Westminster Pier and talked to the officer in charge. He says they found some dope in the pockets so they ran his prints through the files. It's Berry all right.'

Raven took a sip from the glass of juice by the bed,

still trying to pull himself together. 'Did anyone see him go in?'

'Apparently not. It was foggy in any case. They did the post-mortem last night. There were no signs of any external injuries. The inquest's at Horseferry Road at half-past eleven this morning.'

'That soon? I thought it took longer than that,' said Raven.

'They've got a new coroner down there and he likes to keep things moving along. It seems that this is routine.'

Raven yawned. It was twenty past nine by the travelling-clock on the dressing-table. 'Thanks for telling me. I'll talk to you later.'

It was Mrs Burrows' day off. Raven's way of making the bed was straightening the pillows and duvet. He took the Sony portable into the bathroom and listened to LBC *Newstalk* as he shaved in the tub. There were reports of various fog-related incidents. Cases of motorway pile-ups and hypothermia; nothing about a body being pulled out of the river. The thought of breaking the news of Berry's death to Mallory was disturbing but there was no point in keeping it secret. Raven dried himself in a bath-sheet and pulled on his cords and sweater. He rolled the sitting-room curtains back, revealing a uniform expanse of cheerless grey sky. It was low tide and the gulls swooped over the mud-banks, scavenging for refuse. He collected the post and newspapers from the box at the foot of the steps and wrote a cheque for his yearly mooring-fees. With April coming up, the bills would be flooding in with each delivery. It had been a good year for him, thanks to his broker advising an investment in Eurobonds.

He ate a couple of soft-boiled eggs, leaving the white as usual, and read the newspapers. At twenty past ten he called a radio-cab service. The despatcher promised a cab in five minutes. He pulled on his lumber-jacket and climbed the steps to the Embankment. A black taxi slowed in front of him.

'Horseferry Road Coroner's Court,' said Raven.

The driver made good time as far as Millbank, but then the eastbound vehicles in front started to slow. A truck had shed its load, reducing movement to a single lane. A motor-cycle cop was directing traffic with shrill blasts on his whistle.

The driver turned his head. 'You'd be better off getting out here. It's going to take some time to clear this lot. It won't take you no more than five minutes on foot.'

Raven paid him off and walked past the stalled vehicle. The Coroner's Court was a small, grim-looking building. The entrance was shut. Raven was about to ring the bell when a man emerged from the hallway, carrying a brief-case bearing the initials HMPS.

He shook his head at Raven. 'If it's Nick Berry you're interested in you're too late, I'm afraid. The inquest just finished.'

Raven looked at his watch. 'I was told eleven thirty.'

'Eleven,' the man corrected. His face and manner were kindly. 'Were you a friend of his?'

'An acquaintance. I only met him last week in a pub. We just happened to get talking. He seemed a likeable sort of chap with some interesting stories. He told me he'd left prison the week before.'

'I was his probation officer. There's not a lot we can do for these people, you know. We just don't have the resources. So what brings you here?'

'Curiosity,' said Raven. 'I gave him a few quid to help tide him over. Then someone told me he'd been drowned. What was the verdict?'

'Death by misadventure. The Coroner wanted to know if I could shed any light on Nick's circumstances. But I'm like you, I only met him once when he made his report. There were only three other witnesses. The police officer who found the body, the doctor who did the post-mortem and a man from forensic who proved identity.'

Raven's expression was sympathetic. 'Do you know if he had any family or friends?'

'Not a soul,' said the man. 'His wife divorced him a few months after his conviction and he had no friends. An all too familiar story, I regret.'

'What about the funeral?' asked Raven.

'There's a charity that takes care of that.' The man lifted his briefcase. 'I have the Coroner's release. It's a sad waste of a human life.'

A taxi took Raven to Elm Park Mansions. He used Mallory's keys to let himself into the dark hallway and made the long climb up the stairs. He unlocked Mallory's flat and went into the sitting-room. A small red light glowed on the answering-machine. He touched the control button. A woman's voice sounded in the speaker.

'This is Lucy, it's nine o'clock, Tuesday morning. I couldn't get in touch earlier. I will explain when I see you. The good news is that I think I have found a way out of our difficulty. I want you to meet me in Brompton Oratory at six o'clock this evening. You will see me waiting inside the main entrance near the Baptistery. You must bring those papers with you. Do that and I promise our troubles are over. Six o'clock with the papers, remember!'

Raven adjusted the controls and pressed the replay button. Then he sat on the couch and concentrated. He opened his eyes when the tape stopped again. Lucy's voice was unnatural. She spoke without ellipses or hesitation. Each word was given the same amount of stress. It wasn't a normal speech pattern, more like someone reading from a script.

He lifted the phone and reached Mallory at the Danforth Apartments. 'I'm in your flat,' he said. 'There's a message on your answering-machine. Listen to it.'

He held the mouthpiece close to the machine and reran the tape. 'Is that Lucy's voice?' he asked.

Mallory sounded bewildered. 'Yes. It's her right enough.'

'Don't move,' Raven instructed. 'I'm on my way over.'

He put the tape in his pocket and hurried down to the street. Mallory's car was still parked in front of the church. A cab took Raven to Hans Crescent. Mallory answered the bell. Raven pushed into the room and shut the door. 'This is going to come as a shock,' he warned. 'Nick Berry's been drowned. His body was found in the river yesterday. I've just come from the Coroner's Court. I got there too late for the hearing but I spoke to Nick's probation officer. The verdict was death by misadventure. I know what this means to you, Martin, but it's better you know the truth.'

Mallory's face turned the colour of putty. He sank on the bed, his lips working soundlessly. Tears welled in his eyes. He groped for his handkerchief.

Raven spoke with quick sympathy. 'The probation officer's taking care of the funeral arrangements. You've got to be strong, Martin. Nick's out of your life. There's nothing more you can do for him.'

Mallory raised his head. 'Do you think they know about me?'

'Not a word,' replied Raven. 'Your name wasn't mentioned. The problem is Lucy. I've got a bad feeling about this tape. It doesn't sound right to me. If you've got the ear, you can detect it. I'm pretty sure she was reading from a piece of paper with someone standing beside her.'

A vacuum cleaner droned in the hallway outside. Raven lowered himself on to a chair.

'We're going to keep this appointment. Lucy won't be there but somebody will. The Oratory will be full of people attending six o'clock Mass. There's no question of any violence. I'll be right there with you. We'll leave nothing to chance. I'll go to the Oratory and check things out. Make sure of all the exits before we go there tonight.'

Mallory put his handkerchief back in his pocket. 'I'll do whatever you say. I won't let you down, you can count on it.'

'We've got no choice,' said Raven. 'I know this isn't

going to be easy for you but we've got to get these bas-
tards out in the open; it's our only chance.'

Mallory's eyes held a hint of defiance. 'As long as you're
there, I can do it.'

'I'm sure you can. We're in this together, Martin.
Remember that. I'll be back here at five, OK?'

Raven walked home along the Embankment. There
were no messages on his machine. He quick-fried a bowl
of risotto and drank some beer. Only time would tell if
Mallory's change of heart was more than bravado.

It was after three when he drove the Orion on to the
forecourt in front of the Priest's House. It was logical to
assume that there was a way into the Oratory but he had
to be certain. He peered through the glass-fronted door
to the hallway. Statues of saints stood at the foot of a
staircase hung with religious paintings. A curtain hung
in the corridor on his right. The door clicked open
suddenly.

An elderly priest emerged from a side-room, adjusting
his soutane. He spoke with an Irish accent. 'I was watching
you from the window. If it's confession you're wanting,
I'm the duty-father.'

'I was trying to get into the Oratory,' said Raven, 'but
I seem to have lost my way.'

The priest looked at him shrewdly. 'Are you a
Catholic?'

The question took Raven off guard. He said the first
thing that came to mind. 'Lapsed, I'm afraid.'

'Ah, there's no such thing,' the priest said, smiling. 'Just
people in need of prayer. Jesus broke bread for the sinner
as well as the saint, remember. I'll let you into the Oratory. It's peaceful in there, a whole lot better than standing
here listening to me blethering.'

He took Raven's arm in a friendly grasp and walked
him through the curtain in front of them. He unfastened
the Yale lock on the door at the end of the corridor.

'God go with you, my son. And say a little prayer
for me.'

Raven knelt in the nearest pew and covered his eyes with interlaced fingers, self-absolved of any feeling of guilt. A stranger had offered his hand in friendship. It was as basic as that.

He came to his feet. Visitors were scattered in groups near the side-chapels. He crossed the broad nave into the shadows behind the organ-gallery and walked slowly towards the front of the building. There were only three ways in and out of the Oratory, the side-door he had come through and the two main entrances. He located the Baptistery. An ormolu lamp hung unlit above an octagonal font. A curtained confessional stood near the wall. Side-tables offered a variety of tracts and votary candles.

Raven descended six steps into daylight. The bookshop attached to the porch closed at five. He turned left towards a padlocked pathway between the Oratory and the driveway that led to the neighbouring Protestant church. There were a couple of ramps in the driveway where lime trees displayed their first buds.

Raven strolled on. Saint Jude's Church stood at the end of the driveway, an early Victorian building badly in need of restoration. The public garden at the rear had trees and benches. Half a dozen cars were parked on an expanse of tarmac behind a cantilevered pole blocking the entrance. An arrowed sign indicated a basement reception area. The two women inside suspended their conversation as Raven appeared.

He leaned over the counter. 'Good afternoon! I wonder if you ladies could help me. Is this church in use?'

They looked at one another for a moment before the older woman spoke. 'Suzie's the best one for that. She's the vicar's sister.'

Her companion was forty years younger with a straight fall of chestnut hair, a towelling top and a pair of tennis shorts.

'I'm Suzie Malkus,' she said pleasantly. 'Are you new in the neighbourhood?'

'No,' he said. 'I live in Chelsea. A friend of mine mentioned your church but I wasn't sure I'd found the right place.'

His eyes lodged on the car park beyond the windows. A grey squirrel dropped from a sign prohibiting dogs, ball games and radios, and scampered under a car.

She smiled. 'Saint Jude's was reconsecrated two years ago but services are being held in the church hall until the building's restored.' She offered a pamphlet. 'This'll tell you something about our activities.'

He glanced at it briefly. ' "Charismatic"? I'm not sure what that means in terms of religion.'

She lifted a flap in the counter. 'We're a liberal church with C of E beliefs. Would you like me to show you round?'

'If it wouldn't be too much trouble,' said Raven.

She led him up an open staircase to the floor above, indicating the bare supporting beams. 'The church hadn't been used since the end of the war. We've still got a long way to go, I'm afraid.'

A wooden stage served as an altar. There was a plain brass crucifix and an electric keyboard on the bare boards. A pile of dismantled pews lay under the stained-glass windows, a carpenter's bench near the nail-studded door at the other end of the church. She dragged the door open.

'We try to get everyone involved in our worship. One of the group that plays here writes our songs. Do you like contemporary music?'

'Some of it,' he said.

She pointed beyond the wire fence enclosing the gardens behind the car park. There was a long brick building there with wide windows.

'That's the church hall. We live in the house next to it.'

A pathway led from the hall to the car park.

Her hair swung as she cocked her head. 'It doesn't look much, I know. I think the best way to judge would be to see for yourself if you're really interested. There's a musical service tonight.'

'What time?' he asked.

She hunched a shoulder. 'Any time after six. It's all very informal. Do you get along with young people?'

'How old do you think I am?' he said.

She considered him carefully. 'I'm not sure. I've never been good at guessing men's ages. Thirty-eight?'

'You're flattering me,' he said. Then, nodding at the cars, he asked, 'Is there room to park?'

'As long as you get here early. The barrier's lifted at five o'clock. Those cars you see belong to people with permits. It all goes to help the restoration fund.'

It was all he needed to know. 'Then I may see you later.'

She widened her smile. 'I hope so. You'll be very welcome.'

Raven retrieved his car and drove to Hans Crescent. He rang the bell. Mallory let him in and switched off the television set. His pony-tail was neatly tied and he was wearing a clean dark-blue shirt.

Raven shifted a Harrods shopping-bag and sat on the end of the bed.

'How do you feel?'

Mallory's face showed a look of determination. 'A lot better. I've been doing some thinking. I'm sick of being pushed around.'

Raven nodded approval. 'This is the plan. There's no way of knowing who'll be there. My guess is that there'll be more than one and they'll probably come in a car. There's another church behind the Oratory. That's where we'll park. We'll just have to play it by ear from then. But don't worry, I won't let you out of my sight.'

Neither man spoke as they drove west along the Brompton Road. The stores were still open, passengers waiting at the bus-stops. Traffic was heavy in both directions. Raven waited his chance to filter right on to the approach lane to Saint Jude's. He slowed as he neared the ramps. The barrier was raised in front of the empty parking-space. He backed the car in close to the barrier and turned off the engine. The church hall was lit.

'I'll leave the doors unlocked,' he said quietly. 'You know what to do if we're separated. Just make sure you're not followed and head back here and wait for me. I'll do the rest.'

A minibus trundled over the ramps and stopped twenty yards away. A group of teenagers clambered out and disappeared into the church hall. Raven waited until the door closed behind them. 'Let's get going.' They walked up the driveway. Cars and taxis were pulling up in front of the Oratory.

'Go right,' ordered Raven. He was a few steps behind. The congregation was shuffling in, the women with their heads covered. Tall ceremonial candles blazed on the High Altar. More candles flickered in the side-chapels. The atmosphere was heavy with the pungency of incense. Strains of organ music swelled from the gallery.

Raven slid into a pew at the back. People were still coming in. He kept his eyes on Mallory. The curtains parted in the confessional. A man in a black leather jacket emerged, crossing himself. He approached Mallory and spoke to him. There was too much noise for Raven to hear what he said but Mallory's face showed no alarm. The two men moved towards the exit, Raven followed.

A grey hatchback drew up outside. The man at the wheel reached back and opened the rear door. Mallory showed the first sign of concern, resisting the command to get into the hatchback. Car horns sounded impatiently. Raven surged forward. The full weight of his body sent the man sprawling to the ground. Raven ran hard for the driveway. Mallory was twenty yards ahead. Raven caught him up as headlamps turned after them. The hatchback hit the first ramp at speed, shattering one of the headlamps. Raven wrenched the Orion's door open. Mallory climbed in next to him.

The men in the hatchback were straightening the damaged wing. They appeared to be arguing. Then a door slammed and the hatchback reversed and disappeared into the traffic.

'Did you manage to get the numbers?' said Raven.

'I had other things on my mind,' answered Mallory.

'They'd probably be false in any case,' said Raven. 'I got a good look at both of them. Let's get out of here quickly.'

He put the car in motion. Broken glass shimmered on the driveway. He turned left on to Brompton Road and stopped in front of the Danforth Apartments. Harrods was closed; Hans Crescent was empty except for a few window-shoppers.

Raven put his hand on Mallory's knee. 'I'm proud of you, Martin.'

Mallory mopped his neck with his handkerchief. 'So what happens now?'

Raven looked at him carefully. 'You realize what this means? Those men have got hold of Lucy. I keep coming back to Lambert. Is there any way I can enrol as a student?'

Mallory's voice was uncertain. 'Are you serious?'

'I've got to get in there somehow,' said Raven. 'I've got this feeling that Lambert knows more than he's saying.'

Mallory hunched his shoulders doubtfully. 'There's what they call the Introductory Course. I don't know how it works exactly. But you get a month's board and lodging, then it's up to you if you want to continue.'

Raven pressed on. 'Where do you make the application?'

'The Bursar,' said Mallory. 'But I'll tell you this much. You'll come across some very odd people there. A lot of them live in a world of their own.'

This was a new Mallory talking, a man with a chip on his shoulder. 'You're safe for the moment,' said Raven. 'And I'll be in constant touch. Just don't go out any more than you have to.'

'I won't,' said Mallory. 'And don't worry about me. I can take care of myself.'

Raven drove back to Chelsea Embankment. Water was lapping the foot of the steps. A lamp shone on Lauterbach's boat. It was an ex-RN MTB with the diesel engine and controls ripped out, making room for two large cabins, kitchen and shower-stall and Elsan toilet. What had been the wheelhouse was now the lounge. A dog barked as Raven reached the gangway. The door at the top swung open.

Lauterbach was a rangy six-footer in his early thirties with a light-brown brushtop, wearing jeans and a sweat-shirt bearing the device UCLA. He was holding a half-eaten chicken leg in one hand and used the other in greeting. A brindled Great Dane lying on the floor thumped its tail amiably as Raven entered. Lauterbach aimed the chicken bone at the river and kicked the door shut. Thick glass portholes sealed in the warmth from a bottled-gas heater. There was a large bunk spread with a stained cellular blanket and a short-wave radio on a ledge overhead. Lauterbach made a habit of tuning in to police frequencies.

'Is this a social visit,' he said, 'or are you going to bitch about the noise we made last night?'

Raven picked a few dog hairs from the blanket and leaned back against the bulkhead. 'I need a favour.'

Lauterbach reversed a chair and straddled it. 'What sort of favour?'

'There's an outfit in Surrey called the Wycherly Foundation for Religious Studies. I'm taking one of their introductory courses.'

Lauterbach looked like a man told that his flies are undone. 'Are you putting me on?' he demanded.

'I'm serious,' said Raven. 'The thing is, I can't use my own name or address. I need an alias. I was thinking about that cousin of yours. You know, the actor – the one you got that flat for in Covent Garden.'

'He never used it,' said Lauterbach. 'They were supposed to start shooting at Pinewood but the accountants decided it was too expensive and switched the whole deal to Madrid. That's where Brad is at the moment.'

'But you've still got the keys?' probed Raven. The two men had known one another for eight years, linked by the same cavalier approach to conventional behaviour. Raven's lifestyle fascinated his neighbour, a flashback to his own questionable past.

'Yeah, I've got the keys,' said Lauterbach. 'What is this? One of your gang-busting exploits?'

'Just asking a simple favour,' said Raven. Lauterbach was in one of his difficult moods and would have to be humoured.

Lauterbach looked at him, wagging his head. 'You're a wild and disruptive individual, do you know that? Full of those wacky ideas about lateral justice and stuff. Life isn't like that, old buddy. We all get a little less than we're due and the rest's up for grabs.'

Raven continued patiently. 'Then there's no reason why I shouldn't use Brad's name and address?'

'You know what pisses me off about you?' said Lauterbach. 'You take me for granted. You came here asking for help four years ago. And what happened? I stuck my neck out for you. I think I deserve to be told a little more.'

'It isn't the moment,' said Raven. 'I'll know more when I've been down to Corton Bassett. If things turn out the way I hope, we'll sit down and have a long talk.'

A look of complicity passed between them and registered. Lauterbach nodded. 'I've only been there once to collect the keys but I can tell you there's no place to park. The address is two hundred and twenty-eight Floral Street. The woman who owns it's a painter. She's staying with her sister in Italy.'

'Is there anyone else in the building?'

'A guy on the top floor, another painter. They both use the flats as studios.'

The two men came to their feet and slapped hands. 'Are you going to be here for a while?' Raven asked.

'I'll tell you what I'm going to do,' Lauterbach said, stretching his long arms. 'I'm going to roll myself a big fat spliff and let my mind dwell on finer things.'

'I'll be back in an hour or so,' said Raven.

He took the Sloane Square Underground, surfaced at Covent Garden and walked round the corner to Floral Street. The number he wanted was opposite a dance school. He opened the front door into the silent hallway and let himself into the flat on the first floor. The walls were draped with lengths of coloured muslin. There was a couch, an unfinished acrylic painting on an easel, blankets and sheets next to the phone on the table. He lifted the receiver and checked the dialling tone then took a quick look in the curtained alcove and saw a shower-stall and lavatory. The refrigerator door was wide open, a pile of out-of-date magazines lying on top. It was perfect, he thought. An address and a telephone which nobody answered. He found a cab to take him home.

Lauterbach opened the cabin door, releasing a cloud of pungent smoke. He offered the joint in his hand. Raven shook his head and returned the keys.

'I'll be gone by the time you're up in the morning. Keep an eye on the boat. If you need me call the Wycherly Foundation. Directory Enquiries will give you the number. You know who to ask for.'

'You got it,' said Lauterbach. 'And don't let them mess with your head.'

Back on his boat, Raven scrambled some eggs and drank a glass of red wine. He put the dirty plate in the sink and wrote a note to Mrs Burrows saying he'd be away for a few days. He left the note on the dresser where she would see it. Then he turned off the sitting-room lights and lay on the sofa. The gentle roll of the barge, the familiar groan of the hawsers lulled him to contemplation. Old memories revived. He had lived too long not to know when to follow his hunches. Instinct told him he had chosen the right direction.

Chapter Six

He woke early, took a quick shower and made himself breakfast. He dressed in his corduroy trousers with a high-necked sweater and a pair of rubber-soled loafers. He took a Gladstone bag from the guest-room and packed a couple of flannel button-down shirts, his electric razor and a thin cotton robe and pyjamas. He added the portable radio. He called the Wycherly Foundation just after nine o'clock and spoke to a girl in the Bursar's Office. She confirmed what Mallory had told him. The Introductory Course cost £500 and the fee was not refundable. He gave her the name Bradley Pinner with the Floral Street address and telephone number and said he'd be there in a couple of hours.

He pulled on his lumber-jacket, carried his bag into the cul-de-sac and opened the car. He threw the bag on the passenger seat and removed the parking-permit from the dashboard. He made sure there was nothing in the car bearing his name or address and unlocked the boot. He tilted the spare wheel on its side, put his burglary tools and parking-permit in the well, and replaced the wheel. He cashed a cheque for five hundred pounds at his bank in Knightsbridge and drove west along Cromwell Road. It was an hour later when he took the turning to Corton Bassett. He followed the signs through the trees and stopped in front of an ornamental iron gate. A man wearing overalls appeared from the lodge. Raven lowered his window and called.

'I'm looking for the Bursar's Office.'

The man opened the gate and pointed up the driveway. 'You'll find it in the main entrance-hall next to the Coffee Shop.'

The Orion jolted over the cattlegrid. There was a half-acre car park in front of the long two-storey building. A dozen cars, including Lambert's Bentley, stood in the space reserved for staff. Raven pulled in behind them and carried his bag into the wide lobby. Lights burned in the corridors and Coffee Shop. He tapped on the door to the Bursar's Office. A girl wearing a mohair dress and a brace on her teeth looked up as Raven came in.

'I'm Bradley Pinner,' he said. 'I think we spoke earlier?'

She spoke into a voice-box. 'Mister Pinner's just arrived. Shall I show him in?' She turned to Raven and smiled. 'The Bursar will see you now.'

The man in the room beyond rose from his desk and offered his hand. His grey hair was arranged to conceal his baldness and he was wearing a brown double-knit sweater. Thick eyebrows crawled like caterpillars when he spoke.

'If you'd like to sit down, we'll get rid of the formalities.'

Raven put his bag on the floor near his chair and unbuttoned his jacket. The window offered a partial view of two low red-brick buildings set among the trees.

'Those are the dormitories,' said the Bursar. He pulled a printed form close and studied it.

'Let's see if we've got the details right. You live at 228 Floral Street, WC2, and you want to enrol on the Introductory Course. I take it you know the conditions?'

Raven nodded. 'Five hundred pounds, non-returnable. I brought the money with me.' He placed ten fifty-pound notes on the desk. The last time he had heard this voice had been through the wall of Lucy's bedroom.

The Bursar counted the notes and wrote a receipt. 'Do you mind me asking how you heard of us?'

Raven had the answer ready. He looked away for a

moment before he replied. 'My wife died fifteen months ago. It was a great shock to me. I've been trying to come to terms with things ever since. You see, my wife was deeply religious and I've always thought of myself as an agnostic. It left me in a moral quandary. I tried various forms of counselling but nothing helped. Then a friend suggested the Wycherly. I decided to see for myself.'

The Bursar clasped his hands together. 'We don't claim miracles but good things do happen here, I can assure you. It's entirely up to you whether you accept or reject anything we teach. There's no curriculum for students taking the Introductory. You're free to come and go as you please. You might find this useful.'

The photocopied sheet of paper he offered contained a sketch of the Foundation, locating the various classrooms, the lecture-room, library and gymnasium. It gave the times of the trains and bus service to London. The lower half of the sheet was printed in upper case.

ALL PERSONAL BELONGINGS REMAIN THE RESPONSIBILITY OF THE OWNER! THE FOUNDATION WILL NOT ENTERTAIN ANY CLAIM FOR COMPENSATION. STUDENTS ARE INVITED TO BEHAVE TOWARDS ONE ANOTHER IN A SPIRIT OF LOVE AND CHARITY.

The Bursar smiled. 'It doesn't always work but you'll find us reasonably civilized. Do you like talking to people?'

'That depends,' said Raven. 'I can be a good listener if I find the conversation interesting.'

'I'll tell you why I ask,' said the Bursar. 'We've got a mixture of all kinds of people and backgrounds. Most of them have a story to tell.'

'Is there anyone else doing the same course as me?' asked Raven.

'Just the one at the moment.' The Bursar opened the door and spoke to the girl in the outer office. 'I'd like you to show Mister Pinner his quarters, Hilary. I told the housekeeper to give him a room at the back.'

'I've got the key,' she replied, smiling at Raven.

It was quiet in the gardens outside. The girl's heels clicked on the pathway as she struggled to match Raven's long strides. She opened the door into a lobby with a bulletin board near a couple of pay phones. The girl led the way down a corridor and put the key in a lock. 'You'll find there's a rush for the bathroom before eight in the morning and after supper. But they're empty during the day.'

The room had a raw-pine table and wardrobe, a mirror over the hand-basin. Sage-grey curtains matched the carpet. The single bed faced the window. A notice was pinned to the back of the door.

NO VISITORS TV OR RADIO AFTER 11 PM

The girl looked from the bed to Raven's long body. He tried the mattress and grinned.

'That seems OK. If it's good enough for the rest of me, my feet won't complain.'

The brace on her teeth made her look younger. 'I hope you find peace here,' she said. 'Goodbye, Mister Pinner.'

She waved and was gone. He unpacked his bag and put his radio on the small table. A week should be long enough for his purpose. Meanwhile he was hungry.

He strolled back to the main building. The classrooms were busy. The Coffee Shop was the size of a tennis-court with two large windows overlooking the car park. The walls were decorated with murals depicting mankind embroiled with the forces of nature. Two waitresses dressed in gingham uniforms were talking behind a serving counter. The menu was chalked on a blackboard. There was a choice between shrimps and water chestnuts cooked with brown rice, roast pork with dumplings and onion, or vegetable lasagne.

All but two of the tables were empty. A couple of

Chinese clad in black tunic-suits were leaning forward, pushing food into their mouths with chopsticks. The woman sitting alone at the other table looked in her early forties. She was dressed in a lavender cashmere sweater and designer jeans and wore a pair of dark glasses pushed up on her long auburn hair.

Raven moved to the counter. 'I'll take the shrimps and the rice, please.'

The waitress started filling his plate. 'Can I have your room number, please.'

He gave it and glanced at the cooler. 'And a Coke.'

The waitress stuck a straw in the can and added it to the food on the tray. She spiked his order and resumed her conversation with her colleague.

The woman sitting alone looked up deliberately as Raven carried his tray to a window-table. He ate with his back to her. The meal finished, he pushed his plate aside. A movement behind him drew his attention.

The woman put her coffee-cup on the table. 'Do you mind if I join you?'

He rose a couple of inches, wiping his mouth. 'By all means,' he invited.

She sank down gracefully and crossed her legs at the ankles. She spoke with an American accent. 'I'm Bernadette Brandt.'

'Bradley Pinner,' he said.

Her left hand sported a cabochon emerald. Her eyes were ringed with dark circles. 'I haven't seen you before.'

'I only arrived an hour ago,' he said.

She considered him gravely. 'And what brought you here, Mister Pinner?'

He reached for his cigarettes and saw the no-smoking sign.

'Uncertainty, loneliness,' he said. 'My wife passed away suddenly last year. It left me with a lot of doubts in my mind.'

'I know the feeling only too well,' she said, wafting her

scent in his direction. 'I've been through it myself. Carl – my husband – died four years ago and I've been looking for the answers ever since. Are you a religious man, Mister Pinner?'

He decided that this was no more than genuine interest. 'I believe God's like Santa Claus: he exists if you believe in him.' He smiled to take the cynicism out of the words. 'Faith's what I'm looking for.'

She rushed a quick apology. 'If I'm being pushy, just say so.'

'Not at all,' he replied. 'I'm glad to have someone to talk to.'

Her smile showed perfect teeth. 'Do you live in England?'

'In London,' he said. 'How about you?'

'Me? I'm a gypsy. We had this ranch in the Carmel Valley. I sold it when Carl died. He was a musician, you see, and the house was too full of memories. I've been travelling ever since. Have you spent any time in India?'

'No. I don't think I could handle the heat and the poverty.'

She watched as the two Chinese vacated their table. Mrs Brandt opened her handbag and used a lipstick. She rolled her lips and blotted them on a tissue. 'I spent six months in an ashram. I left there totally disillusioned. This place hasn't been any better. I came here like you, hopefully. I'm leaving tomorrow.'

'That's too bad,' he said politely.

The door from the hallway opened on a good-looking white-haired man in a dark business-suit. He spoke to one of the waitresses then his eyes found Raven's table. He lifted a hand in greeting.

'Bernadette! What time are you off in the morning?'

She looked like a cat about to be mauled by a mastiff. 'Early enough to avoid you, I hope.'

The man showed no trace of discomfiture. 'Well, peace go with you in any case.'

They watched him drive the Bentley away.

'That was Ludovic Lambert, the Principal,' said Mrs Brandt. 'Have you met him yet?'

Raven shook his head slowly.

'You will,' she said darkly. 'He sees everyone sooner or later.'

The edge on her voice encouraged him. 'He looks pleasant enough.'

'Oh, he is,' she replied. 'He's a total hypocrite.' The waitresses were giggling behind the counter. Mrs Brandt's gesture drew him closer. 'This isn't a pick-up,' she said, 'but I need to talk to you. Can you have a drink with me later this evening?'

The urgency in her voice fired his curiosity. 'I'd like that,' he said. 'Where should we meet?'

She pointed across the car park at the tree-lined lane beyond. 'There's only one cottage, you can't miss it. I'll leave the light on. About eight thirty?'

'That'll be fine,' he said. 'Would you like me to bring a bottle?'

'No,' she replied. 'I've got vodka and whisky and I think there's some wine left.'

He turned his watch on his wrist. 'You'll have to excuse me,' he said, pulling his chair back. 'I still have to get my bearings.'

Her eyes held on his face. 'Then I'll see you later.'

It was dark when Raven drove into Corton Bassett. He bought a large bunch of tulips from the shop next to the market-garden, had a quick meal in a café and headed back to the Foundation. He left the Orion in the empty car park, took the bunch of flowers from the passenger seat and started walking down the lane. Scarred beech trees pressed in from both sides. An electrified storm-lantern lit the front of a red-brick bungalow standing in a clearing between the trees and the river. A stub of chimney thrust through the tiled roof. The curtains had been drawn shut but the front door was ajar. The sound of George Shearing's blocked piano-chords came from inside.

Raven stepped into a candle-lit room with cream-stuccoed walls and a fake beam ceiling. A wood fire blazed in the open hearth. A deep sofa was positioned in front of the fireplace. A table was set with glasses, slices of lemon and an ice bucket, and two bottles. The Scotch was untouched, the vodka half-empty. He placed the tulips on the table beside them.

Mrs Brandt emerged from the bedroom. Her hands flew to her heart as she saw the flowers.

'For *me*?' she cried. 'I can't believe it! Nobody's given me flowers in years.'

Her voice was slurred. She had clearly been drinking. 'Just a promise of spring,' he said lightly.

She cradled the flowers in her arms. 'I'll put them in water,' she said. 'Fix yourself a drink and give me a vodka.'

There was no tonic water. He refilled her glass, covering the ice-cubes with vodka, and poured himself a Scotch. Mrs Brandt returned from the kitchen carrying a vase that she placed on a table in front of the French windows at the end of the room.

She sat down beside him. 'That was a very sweet thought and I'm touched.' She put her head on one side and looked at him. 'Do you think I'm drunk, Mister Pinner?'

'You've had a couple,' he said guardedly.

'Well, I am,' she replied. She emptied her glass deliberately and assessed his reaction. 'We probably won't ever see one another again. That makes it easy to speak my mind. But if you don't want to hear it just say so.'

'If you want to talk, I'm happy to listen,' he said.

She tilted the vodka bottle. The emerald flashed as she poked the ice with a manicured forefinger.

'Do you know what it's like, realizing that you've been deceived, Mister Pinner?'

Her mood seemed to change without warning.

'I've known it happen,' he said.

She took a cigarette from the pack of Gitanes on the table and used his Dupont to light it. She took one drag on the strong black tobacco and threw the cigarette into the flames.

'I'm not a cynic, you know. I'm a sensitive woman who came here like you, in search of an answer – peace of mind, if you like.'

The set of her mouth, her eyes, told him there was more to come. 'I'm sorry it didn't work out,' he said.

'You're sorry,' she mocked. 'What the hell would you know about it! You're light-years away from what I've been through.'

'I'm doing my best,' he said defensively.

She refused to be mollified. 'Then listen,' she snapped. She drank what remained in her glass, unabashed. 'I came here with an open mind, naïve if you like. I wanted to put my experiences down on paper, get some sort of shape in my thinking. Do you see anything wrong in keeping a diary?'

'I've never kept one myself, but no.'

'That's what I thought,' she said. 'So I wrote about my life here, the things that didn't make sense to me.'

The music came to an end abruptly. The room was silent except for the crackle of logs and the sound of the river beyond the French windows.

Mrs Brandt's fingers were trembling. 'Someone came in here and read my diary. It was in my bedroom when I went to the Coffee Shop. I came back here and found that the drawer had been opened. A woman senses these things.'

'It's an unpleasant feeling,' he said.

'I threw that diary straight on the fire,' she said. 'It was like having something filthy in my hands, you know, as if I'd been caught doing something foul.'

'I think that's ridiculous,' he said. 'What on earth could you have written to be ashamed of?'

She pushed a hand through her auburn hair. 'Nothing. They were just, you know, *thoughts*. Questions I was asking myself, stuff that occurred to me. Then the next day there was this man watching the cottage from the other side of the river. I've never seen him before. So I went out and told him that he was on private property. He just walked away without even answering.'

'Didn't you tell anyone?'

'I spoke to Lambert,' she said. 'I told him that someone had been in my bedroom and I told him about the man who'd been watching the cottage. Do you know what he did? He laughed at me! He accused me of being neurotic. He said that nobody'd be interested in my diary. He told me there was a right of way through the wood to the road, that it was a route hikers often used.'

Raven put his suggestion peaceably. 'Don't you think he might have been right?'

'No,' she asserted. She was lying. 'And I'll tell you something else. Those two Chinese men we saw in the Coffee Shop. The Foong cousins. They've been here for four months without putting a foot in the classrooms. They never speak to anyone else, just stay in their rooms or play ping-pong. A limo collects them every Friday and they're back here on Sunday.'

He smiled in spite of himself. 'Is that what you wrote in your diary?'

'Don't laugh at me,' she cautioned. 'I think it's drugs.'

'Did you say that to Lambert?'

Her look was impatient. 'Of course not. I don't want to put my life in danger.'

There was no doubt that she meant what she said. 'Then why don't you go to the police?' he asked.

She looked at him scornfully. 'Have you any idea at all what I've been talking about? A foreigner accusing a man like Lambert? What proof do I have?'

'None,' he replied. 'And I mean this kindly. I think you've been under a lot of emotional stress and you're blowing this thing up way out of proportion. I don't think this place is good for you.'

She lurched to her feet and flung the front door wide. 'Thank you for the flowers, Mister Bradley Pinner. I hate to have to tell you this but you're full of crap. Now I'll thank you to get out of my house.'

He paused in the doorway. 'Good night, Mrs Brandt. I've enjoyed your company.'

The door slammed and the light overhead was extinguished, leaving him in total darkness. He picked his way through the trees to the dormitory. He read the names on the board in the vestibule. The Foongs occupied adjoining rooms a few yards along the corridor. A typewriter clattered in one of them. It was still early but Raven was tired. A note had been slipped under his door: *Please come to my office at 2.15 tomorrow. L. Lambert, Principal.*

Raven brushed his teeth, donned his pyjamas and thought about Bernadette Brandt. She was a bruised, lonely woman with a serious drink problem. He felt he had handled her badly. He should have encouraged her to talk more about her relationship with Lambert. As things were she'd be gone in the morning. If the Foongs kept to their weekly routine there'd be a chance to look through their rooms.

Raven's main interest was in Lambert. The pivotal question remained why he hadn't reported the theft from his safe. The possibility of blackmail gathered strength in Raven's mind. The men Nick Berry had left the house with might have realized the value of what had been stolen. They'd reason that only two people could know where the missing file was. Lucy and Mallory. And the file was sitting in Raven's writing-desk.

Chapter Seven

The cleaners were finishing their work when Raven left his room and walked up the pathway towards the main building. The Foong cousins were waiting in front of the entrance, dressed in dark suits, one of them holding a portable telephone. Raven went into the deserted Coffee Shop. He ordered tea and toast and sat at the window. A limousine drew up minutes later. The two Chinese got in the back and the hire-car glided away.

Raven finished his breakfast and strolled down the lane to the bungalow. It looked smaller by daylight. Refuse-bags had been left near the front door for collection. He looked through the sitting-room window. The fire was relaid, the vase of flowers removed. The bungalow awaited its next occupant.

Raven returned to the car park and undid the boot of his car. He made a show of inspecting the spare wheel and slipped the small box of tools into his lumber-jacket pocket. He shut the boot again. The lights were on in the classrooms and first-floor offices. He let himself into the silent dormitory, took a Yale master-key from the box and unlocked the door in front of him. He thumbed the button up, rendering the spring-loaded lock immovable and glanced round the room. A pair of matching Samson-ite suitcases was standing against the wall. He looked in the wardrobe. There were four shelves and a recess for hanging garments. Three hand-stitched suits were sus-pended on plastic forms. A Kowloon tailor's label was sewn inside the jackets. Behind the suits was an Italian anorak lined with fur-fabric. There was an array of silk shirts, expensive underwear and shoes. He shut the wardrobe and opened the larger suitcase. There was nothing inside. The smaller bag was locked. He took a probe like a crochet needle from his tool-kit and inserted it delicately into the lock. He swivelled his wrist and felt the levers rise. He viewed a Hong Kong passport and a quantity of US dollars. He read the letter tucked into the upper flap. It was typed in English on heavy bond paper.

Helmut Klopper Rechtsanswalt
471 Oststrasse
Düsseldorf 1

An Herrn S. Foong
Wycherly Foundation
Corton Bassett
Surrey
United Kingdom

Dear Mr Foong,

In accordance with your recent instructions we have enquired about the property situated am Zoo. The owner is asking a purchase price of DM836,000.

We consider this to be excessive in view of the current recessional house market and have so advised the seller. We are awaiting his reply and shall inform you as soon as we hear from him.

We are aware that your need is urgent and assure you of our wish to be of assistance.

with heartfelt regards
Helmut Klopper

Raven snapped the self-locking catch shut and let himself into the room next door. He found the same display of expensive clothing in the wardrobe, and a Minolta 35mm camera. There was an open suitcase on the bed next to a portable typewriter.

He relocked the room and drove into Corton Bassett. A Norman church dominated the muddy grass in front of the neat thatched cottages. A few youths were kicking a football across the pub car park. Raven walked across to the phone-box and dropped a fifty-pence piece in the slot.

'I may be back sooner than I expected,' said Raven. 'Two questions. Do you know a woman called Bernadette Brandt?'

'Never heard of her,' said Mallory.

'How about the Foong cousins?'

'The two from Hong Kong? I know them by sight but they never attended my lectures.'

'Did your girlfriend ever talk to them?'

'She didn't like them,' said Mallory. 'What's going on down there?'

'I'll tell you later,' said Raven. 'I want you to bury yourself for the next couple of days. And stay off the streets. Things could be happening fast. I have to be sure that I know where you are.'

He put the phone down firmly and crossed the forecourt to the pub. The only person in the bar was the landlord, standing behind the counter engrossed in a crossword puzzle. He glanced up at Raven, scratching the side of his face.

'You don't happen to know what "zibbeline" means, do you?'

'I think it's something to do with fur,' said Raven. 'Can I get a meal here?'

The landlord inserted the word and nodded at a glass dome enclosing a pile of sandwiches.

'Ham, cheese or liver sausage. They're all fresh, I cut them this morning.'

'Give me the cheese with a half-pint of Guinness,' said Raven.

The landlord drew a head of foam on the beer and put the plate and glass down on a table near the fire.

'You're not local, are you?'

'Just visiting,' said Raven.

It was twenty past two when he drove into the Wycherly car park. The Bentley had been moved a few yards. Raven walked up the stairs and pushed a door marked ADMINISTRATION.

A woman was sitting at a desk inside.

'Bradley Pinner,' he said.

The door to an inner office opened before she could answer. Lambert was wearing a clove carnation in his lapel. He was four inches shorter than Raven with a dimpled chin and a friendly smile. His handshake was warm and firm.

'Come on in, Mister Pinner,' he said expansively.

It was a large room with bronze velvet curtains, Bokhara rugs and elegant furniture. A glass cobra coiled round the ashtray on the arm of the sofa where Raven was sitting.

Lambert perched on a window-ledge, his eyes curious. 'Didn't I see you in the Coffee Shop yesterday talking to Bernadette Brandt?'

'That's right,' agreed Raven. 'She was kind enough to ask me round for a drink.'

Lambert winced. 'I hope she didn't fill your head full of nonsense. I wouldn't want you to get the wrong impression of us.'

'We didn't get the chance to talk,' said Raven. 'I'm afraid the lady was drunk when I got there. I found it embarrassing. I only stayed a few minutes.'

'I should have warned you,' said Lambert. 'Bernadette's a deeply disturbed woman, a fantasist, prey to a vivid imagination. Thank God she's left. She's caused nothing but trouble since she's been here. Anyway, let's talk about you. All I know is what's on the application form.'

Raven dropped his lumber-jacket on the floor and lit a Gitane.

'There isn't a lot to tell. I'm just a man with a personal problem that needs resolving. I've tried just about everything else but my difficulty seems to be a lack of religious belief . . .'

Lambert looked up from twisting his signet-ring. 'Then what on earth brought you to the Wycherly?'

Raven trickled the salt burn of the tobacco through his nostrils. 'It was Martin Mallory's suggestion.'

Lambert's eyes flickered for no more than an instant. 'You mean you know Martin?'

'We've been friends for years,' said Raven.

'Good Lord,' said Lambert, wagging his head. 'What a small world it is. When did you see him last?'

'A couple of weeks ago,' said Raven. 'We were supposed to have supper on Sunday. But a friend of his died from a heart attack and Martin's taking care of the funeral arrangements.'

'He told me,' said Lambert. 'I can't get over you two knowing one another.'

Raven slapped some more paint on his canvas. 'I belong to the Howard League for Penal Reform and Martin used to attend the meetings. That's how we met.'

Lambert's rich baritone deepened. 'Poor Martin. He told me about his bereavement. I've been feeling guilty ever since. I felt I might have sounded offhand. It's been on my mind. I've tried calling his flat but I can't get an answer. Have you any idea where I can get hold of him?'

'I'm afraid not,' said Raven. 'All I know is that he's staying with his friend's family somewhere in Putney. He promised to call me tonight.'

'You mean here?'

'At home,' said Raven. 'I'm going back to London this afternoon. There are some things I have to take care of before I settle in. Shall I tell Martin you want to talk to him?'

'No,' Lambert said quickly. 'He's got enough on his mind as it is. As long as he knows he can take all the time he needs. When can we expect you back here?'

'I can't be sure,' said Raven. 'Probably on Monday or Tuesday.'

Lambert slid from the window-ledge. 'I've just had a thought. We could put you in the cottage Mrs Brandt was in. You'd have the river near by, the woods to walk in. You'd be completely on your own with no one to bother you. How do you feel about that?'

'It sounds fine to me,' smiled Raven.

'Good,' said Lambert. 'I don't want you to think that I'm interfering but peace of mind isn't always easy to come by, especially for someone in your position. If you ever feel in need of unburdening yourself, just tell me.'

Raven extinguished his cigarette in the ashtray and picked up his lumber-jacket. 'It's been a great help talking to you, Mister Lambert. I'll make sure that Martin gets your message and see you next week.'

Lambert came to the door with him and spoke to the woman outside. 'Tell the Bursar to keep the river cottage free. Mister Pinner may be moving in.'

Raven went back to his room. The interview with Lambert had convinced him of the guile behind the bland charm. A plausible natural scoundrel, Raven decided. His mention of Mallory had been a deliberate attempt to provoke a reaction. The way Lambert had fielded it, the show of commiserative interest proved only one thing to Raven. The next move would come from Lambert.

It was late afternoon when Raven parked in the cul-de-sac. The shop was still closed. Raven was drawing the sitting-room curtains when Lauterbach came through the door, wearing a checked flannel shirt, jeans and sneakers with his socks around his ankles.

'Hey!' he said, coming towards Raven behind an outstretched finger. 'I've been calling you at the Wycherly. Some woman said you were coming back to London and I heard your car. Did you lock up when you left Floral Street?'

'The flat?' Raven cast his mind back. 'Uhuh! I'm pretty sure of it, why?'

'The guy living upstairs. He says that Brad's door was open. I told him that I'd dropped by to see if there was any post for Brad and must have forgotten. He banged on a bit about the need for security and we left it at that. I thought I should tell you.'

Raven had a quick sense of foreboding. 'Shit!' he said. 'I've got a good idea who was there.'

'You want to share it?' said Lauterbach, taking a seat on the sofa.

Raven dropped in his chair. It was a relief to unburden himself. He spent the next half-hour giving an account of his meeting with Mallory and the events of the last few days. He lifted his palms in the air.

'And that's why I went to the Wycherly.'

Lauterbach had been listening with rapt attention, his eyes glinting behind his spectacles.

'All that and you never said one word to me?'

Raven had a quick twinge of conscience. 'I wasn't sure what I was getting into. It's different now. I've opened a whole can of worms. These people are villains.'

'And Mallory's a friend of yours?'

'Not even that,' said Raven. 'He's just a weakling who's got himself deep in trouble. It isn't him I'm thinking about, it's the rest of it. I think it's blackmail.'

Lauterbach loosed a long low whistle and hitched up his socks. 'And you've no idea where Lucy is?'

'No,' said Raven. 'Just the message on Mallory's answering-machine. And the fact that those two charmers turned up at the Oratory. I think they're holding her somewhere.'

'And you want me in on this with you. Is that what you're saying?'

'I *need* you,' said Raven.

'Know what I think?' Lauterbach said. 'I think we could get our asses kicked here.'

'Anything's possible,' said Raven. 'Are you with me or not?'

'What do you think?' said Lauterbach, rubbing his hands together. 'Two heads are better than one,' he said, grinning. 'So what's the scenario?'

There were three things in life that Lauterbach held dear. His dog, his girlfriend and his Harley-Davidson. Raven was never sure about the order of their importance.

'Is your bike working?'

'Buddy, it's always working,' said Lauterbach.

Raven leaned forward, weighing his words. 'This is a leap in the dark, I'll admit. I believe those two jokers are going to turn up at Mallory's flat looking for him some time this evening. If that's right, I'm pretty sure they'll be in a car. Your job's to follow them on your bike and find out where they go. And don't let them out of your sight until they've settled.'

'Got it,' said Lauterbach and consulted his watch. 'It's twenty to six. When do we meet?'

'Seven o'clock, in front of the pub at the bottom of Park Walk. It'll be dark by then and that's what they'll wait for.'

'No problem,' Lauterbach said, rising. 'I'll give Daisy a run and I'll see you there.'

It was twenty to seven when Raven closed the sitting-room door. A cold wind was ruffling the river. He pulled up his collar and walked north towards the Fulham Road.

Lauterbach was standing outside the school opposite the pub, sinister in a one-piece biking suit, a moulded vinyl helmet, gauntlets and thigh-boots. The Harley-Davidson was propped against the kerb.

Raven nodded across at the pub. 'We'll be able to watch the street from upstairs.'

Lauterbach tucked his helmet under his arm. There was a payphone on the left of the long crowded bar. The noise of a jukebox thumped through the babble of conversation.

No one turned a head as the two men pushed through to the stairs leading up to the floor above. A sign on the banister read:

FLAXMAN PLAYERS PRESENT JOE ORTON'S *LOOT* AT 8 P.M.
TICKETS ON SALE AT THE DOOR! NO SMOKING OR
DRINKING DURING PERFORMANCES

Raven paused at the head of the stairs. Wall brackets lit the makeshift theatre. The safety curtain was lowered, collapsible chairs stacked in front of it. They positioned themselves at the window. There was a clear view of the street in both directions. A lamp standard illuminated the entrance to Elm Park Mansions. Time stretched as they waited. Then a grey hatchback turned into the one-way street and stopped behind the line of parked cars. The driver got out and looked up at Mallory's darkened flat. A match flared as he lit a cigarette. Raven's recognition was instantaneous. His grip tightened on Lauterbach's sleeve.

'That's him!'

The man walked back to the cars parked in front of the church, inspecting the number plates until he reached Mallory's Volkswagen. He squatted down by the offside rear wheel and let the air out of the tyre. He repeated the manoeuvre with the other three wheels and spiralled his cigarette into the shadows. The hatchback side-lights came on.

'*Now!*' urged Raven.

The hatchback was thirty yards away when Raven reached the street. The Harley-Davidson was close behind.

Raven moved fast, Mallory's keys in his hand. He climbed the five flights of stairs and let himself into the flat. He sat in the darkness with the phone in his lap. He waited ten minutes before it rang. 'Never rely on the charity of strangers,' said Lauterbach. 'We've just been shafted. You won't believe this. The guy pulled into the Shell station on the corner of Clareville Grove. He filled up with gas and went into the office to pay. Then get this! Someone else drives off in the hatchback. I stuck with the guy in the office. He took a bus to Fulham Broadway and went into some council flats at the bottom of North End Road. That's where I lost him.'

'Where are you now?' said Raven.

'In a pay phone across from the flats.'

'Wait for me,' Raven said hurriedly. A cab dropped him off in Vanston Place. Lauterbach was sitting on his bike watching the block of flats.

'There's isn't another way out,' he told Raven. 'He's got to be in there somewhere.'

Raven looked across the asphalted yard in front of the five-floor building. The flats opened on to exterior corridors. The doors and windows on the bottom floor were boarded up. Dogs had raided the dustbins. A dim light showed in the nearest entrance.

Raven scanned the rows of windows. 'If he's in there we'll find him,' he said.

They crossed the yard, Lauterbach moving in a kind of pimp-roll, his arms dangling loosely. A lamp lit an out-of-order notice on the lift-shaft. The entrance stank of urine. The stone floor was littered with used condoms and disposable syringes.

A man wearing a Rasta bonnet eased off the wall, his hands deep in the pockets of a long camel-hair overcoat.

'Whadda you dudes want?'

Raven had learned how to deal with Rastas. Avoid too much eye contact and show the right amount of savvy and respect.

'We're looking for someone,' he said.

The Rasta jerked a thumb at the yard. 'Piss of!' he said curtly.

Raven maintained his civility. 'That's not a very friendly attitude.'

'It ain't meant to be,' said the Rasta. 'Now piss off before you get hurt.'

Lauterbach took off his gauntlets and stuffed them inside his tunic. His voice was deceptively quiet. 'Didn't you hear what my friend said?'

Raven broke in hastily. 'We don't know his name. He's about your height, thirtyish, with a flat nose and a black leather jacket.'

The Rasta took a fresh look at Lauterbach and spat on the ground. 'I'm a businessman not a fuckin' information service.'

Lauterbach fished in his pocket and held up a ten-pound note. 'I'm a businessman myself.'

'You're barking up the wrong tree, man, if you're looking to score. The geezer you want ain't a dealer but I know someone who is.'

'Just the number of the flat,' said Lauterbach, tendering the note.

The Rasta's hand closed like a vice on the money. 'It's on the second-floor, number thirty-eight. And don't say who told you.'

They watched him take off at a fast clip and vanish across the yard.

'We've got to be careful. He knows me. You'll have to front,' said Raven.

'Cool,' said Lauterbach, smiling. 'You think he's alone?'

Rats scurried in the lift-shaft. 'We'll just have to see. We've got to get that door open somehow. He won't answer unless he's sure who it is. He'll take a good look at you first. Tell him you've got a message from Martin Mallory, OK?'

Lauterbach nodded silently. They climbed the steps, picking their way past a broken bed, a bicycle chained to the railings on the second floor. Raven lifted a hand and they froze. The smell of curry drifted along the corridor. A chest-high parapet extended to their right. The door they wanted was ten feet away. An optic offered a foreshortened view of the corridor outside. Raven flattened his back against the wall as Lauterbach stood in front of the door and rang the bell. A disembodied eye appeared in the spyhole. Lauterbach offered his face for inspection. 'I've got a message from Martin Mallory,' he said.

The eye disappeared. They heard the rattle of a chain being removed. Then the door inched open. Lauterbach burst in, Raven inches behind him. Raven reached the table-drawer before the man in the leather jacket. He grabbed the small six-shot revolver and aimed it. Recognition dawned as the man stared at Raven. He backed off, lifting his hands in the air. Lauterbach pushed the door shut. There was a telephone on the table, a glimpse of a kitchen and bedroom.

'Take your clothes off,' Raven ordered. 'Everything. Then sit on the chair with your hands on your head.'

The man bent slowly and unlaced his shoes. He stripped down to his jockey-shorts, his face set in fear and hostility. He sat on the chair and clasped both hands as instructed. Raven handed the gun to Lauterbach and banged the man's shoes on the floor, making sure that nothing was concealed. Then he went through the man's jacket pockets, placing each item on the table. There was four hundred pounds in fifties, an address-book and a current driving-licence issued in the name of Stephen Armstrong. The trousers netted some loose change, keys and a Metropolitan Police warrant-card. The name on the warrant-card was Detective-Sergeant G. Wainwright. The picture displayed was of the man on the chair.

Raven's practised eye recognized the forgery. He held it up between thumb and forefinger.

'Where'd you get this?'

The man's eyes swivelled in Lauterbach's direction. He made no answer. Raven widened his stance. 'We've met before. At the Oratory, remember?'

The man's tongue snaked over his lips. 'I don't know what you're talking about,' he said sullenly.

Raven placed his hand on the phone. 'Maybe the police will revive your memory. What's your real name?'

'Armstrong.'

'That's better,' said Raven. Honour among thieves was a fantasy. As soon as the cell-door closed they reached for the bell.

'Where'd you get this warrant-card?'

Armstrong's eyes wavered. 'Tel had it done.'

Raven pressed on relentlessly. 'Who's Tel?'

'Terry. My brother-in-law. Look, you've got the wrong bloke,' he pleaded. 'It's him you want, not me. You think I'd have listened to him if I'd known this shit he's got me into? We was skint, mate, and he said we could earn some dosh. I just went along with it.'

'Let's see what we've got here,' said Raven. 'We've got a case of attempted abduction to start with.' He ticked off a second and third finger. 'Impersonating a police officer, and there's the gun. And I'm witness to all of it. I wouldn't give much for your chances. How much form have you got?'

'None. I never been nicked in me life,' Armstrong said stoutly. 'Can I put me arms down? I'm gettin' the bleedin' cramp.'

'Well, watch it,' said Raven. 'My friend gets nervous.'

Armstrong lowered his hands cautiously, his eyes on Lauterbach. 'I dunno who *he* is but I know who you are all right. You're Mallory's friend.'

A cistern was flushed in the flat next door. The television came on.

'Let's talk about something else,' said Raven. 'Nick Berry's landlady said he left the house with two men the morning he drowned. One of them fits your description.'

A flush showed on Armstrong's cheekbones. 'We never laid a finger on him. I didn't even *know* the geezer. He was just an old mate of Terry's. That's why we went to see him.'

Raven was in full flow now. 'What did you talk to Nick about?'

'He told us Mallory give him some keys to this gaff in Chelsea. He said he took some papers out of a safe for Mallory. He said they could be valuable. That's why he wanted to talk to Terry. He said he'd try to find out where the papers were and we made a meet for the following day. But he never turned up. Next thing I heard he'd been drowned. And that's the God's truth, mate.'

'What about the message from Lucy Ashton on Mallory's answering-machine. How did that get there?'

Armstrong showed signs of strain. 'You'd have to ask Terry. He don't tell me nothing no more. I just done what he said. That's what I done all along. He's an animal, mate.'

Raven took a quick glance through the bedroom and kitchen and saw no clothes or food. He thumbed through Armstrong's address-book and found Lambert's number. He closed the book and sat on the edge of the table with the phone in his hand.

'I want you to listen to this conversation. It'll broaden your mind.'

He leaned forward, holding the receiver between them and dialled.

Lambert's rich baritone responded. 'Bradley Pinner,' said Raven.

'Mister Pinner! What a pleasant surprise.'

'I'm in Martin's flat,' said Raven. 'He asked me to see if there was any post for him. There isn't. Not even a message from Lucy.'

'That's Lucy, I'm afraid. I haven't heard either. It really is most inconsiderate. How's Martin coping?'

'He's run off his feet,' said Raven. 'I never realized how much paperwork is involved when somebody dies. I'll tell you why I'm calling you though. There's a message from someone called Armstrong on Martin's machine. He wants Martin to get in touch with him urgently. The thing is, I can't get hold of him at the moment. I was wondering if the name was familiar. Stephen Armstrong?'

'Did he leave a number?'

'Just the message,' said Raven.

Lambert chuckled. 'It's probably one of those scallywags Martin used to visit in prison. I wouldn't let it worry you unduly. Anyway, when are we seeing you back at Corton Bassett? The trees are beginning to bud and the cottage is ready.'

'That depends on Martin. I don't want to leave him alone at the moment.'

'Of course not,' Lambert said quickly. 'But when you do talk, tell him I'll be at Hollywood Mews for the weekend. I'm driving up tomorrow morning. Ask him to call me there.'

'I'll do that,' said Raven.

'And I'll probably see you next week. Bye-bye for now, Mister Pinner, and thanks for calling.'

Raven cradled the handset, smiling. 'I just shopped you,' he said. 'And I wouldn't look for much help from your brother-in-law. You're expendable, as they say in the trade.'

'It's their word against mine,' Armstrong said obstinately.

'You're forgetting me,' replied Raven. 'You're standing on the edge of quicksand. One little push and you're gone.'

Armstrong lifted a stricken face. 'I can't believe this. I cannot believe it!'

Raven turned the screw tighter. 'I've got a real problem with you. You're a liar. So far you haven't given me a single straight answer. You're sly and deceitful. A real piece of shit.'

Armstrong flinched. 'I've got Tel's phone number down in the country. That's got to be worth something.'

Lauterbach was standing close behind Armstrong, still holding the gun.

'Have you got the address?' said Raven.

'Just the number. It's only supposed to be used in an emergency.'

'What is it?' said Raven.

'Zero four two eight, seven three zero, seven four five.' A glimmer of hope showed in Armstrong's eyes. 'What you want me to do?'

'Tell a few more lies,' Raven said curtly. 'Tell him you talked to one of Mallory's neighbours who thinks her husband knows where Mallory's staying. The husband's out at the moment but she's going to ask him as soon as he's back. And make it short.'

He put the phone on Armstrong's knees. Armstrong looked at it as though it might explode.

'It's your only chance,' Raven said sternly.

Armstrong composed the number. His voice had the ring of the fluent liar. 'It's me, Tel! Listen. I just had a word with some woman who lives next to Mallory. She reckons her husband knows where he is. But he ain't there right now. I'm supposed to be calling her later. Whadda you think?'

The Cockney voice sounded clearly. 'Did she seem suspicious at all?'

'Sweet as a nut,' said Armstrong. 'You know, real helpful.'

'Well, watch it,' the voice warned. 'We don't want no more cock-ups. And call me as soon as you've talked to the bloke.'

Armstrong handed the phone to Raven and shuddered.

'Put your clothes on,' said Raven. Armstrong made a locker-room change. Shirt, jacket and shoes then his trousers.

Raven pushed Armstrong's money and driving-licence over the table. 'I'm keeping the address-book and warrant-card.'

He opened the door and glanced down the empty corridor. 'Get out of here before I change my mind.'

Armstrong disappeared like a startled hare. They heard his feet clatter down the staircase, then silence.

Lauterbach unfastened his chin-strap and put his spectacles back on his nose.

'Where do you think he's heading!'

Raven looked around the room with a sense of anticlimax. 'To his brother-in-law. I'm counting on it.'

A slow grin broke on Lauterbach's face. 'I wish I'd had a camcorder. You really get off on that stuff, don't you!'

'We'd better get out of here,' said Raven. 'I'll see you back on the boat – and get rid of the gun.'

It was half an hour later when the cab deposited him on Chelsea Embankment. Lauterbach was standing at the top of the steps, the Great Dane straining against the leash. 'She's bursting,' said Lauterbach.

'Take your time,' said Raven. 'I've got a couple of calls to make in any case.'

He let himself into the civilized warmth of the sitting-room. The answering-machine was blank. He took the phone to the sofa and spoke to Mallory at the Danforth.

'Did Nick Berry see inside the file?'

'He never even opened it. Why?'

'I just wondered,' Raven said casually, unwilling to put fresh strain on the lecturer. 'Is everything else all right?'

'As well as can be expected,' said Mallory. 'Have you been to the flat?'

'Not yet. I haven't had time. I'm back in London. Look, I can't talk now. But things are happening. I'll call you tomorrow, OK?'

He redialled. It was just after three o'clock New York time. A voice said, 'Carlyle Hotel.'

'My name's John Raven. I believe you have my wife staying with you?'

There was a pause while she consulted her screen. 'Yes, sir, we have. Shall I try her room for you?'

Kirstie came on the line. 'You must be psychic. I only got in a few minutes ago. How are you, my darling!'

'Never felt better,' he answered. 'What about you?'

'I'm just fine. I just had lunch with the Fashion Editor and the Art Director. They're thrilled with the shots we took. Isn't that great? There's only the retouching to do and that shouldn't take too long. I ought to be home by the end of next week. Did you go to see Mister Somerton?'

'Yes, I did,' he replied.

'I want to know what he said,' she insisted.

It was Kirstie who had arranged the appointment. Since then she had taken a proprietary interest in his ailment. He reached for the drawer at his elbow. 'I'll read you the letter.'

Dear Mr Raven

I have now got the results of your venous assessment. Your previous operation has proved quite successful although there is indication of perforation in the recurrent varicose vein. This can be treated using mini-stab incisions. These incisions heal without leaving scars. You could come into hospital, have it done, and leave the following day. You would have to wear an elastic stocking for two or three weeks but you can take them off to shower and to wash them. Once you have had the operation the veins could be treated by microsclerotherapy to give a good cosmetic result. There is no urgency for this operation and you could certainly wait until later this year.

Yours sincerely
James Somerton
Consulting Surgeon

'So what are you going to do?' asked Kirstie.

'Nothing,' he said. 'The leg's not troubling me at the moment.'

She giggled. 'You're as stubborn as high hope. And so

vain. It's the thought of the elastic bandage that's worrying you, isn't it?'

'Nonsense,' he said. 'You're the only one who sees me undressed in any case. I've got other things in mind. How about us spending Easter in Paris together?'

She gasped. 'Paris? What a wonderful idea!' she bubbled. I don't know why we never thought of it before. Just the two of us – perfect.'

Her enthusiasm increased his feeling of guilt.

'Then it's settled,' he said. 'As soon as you get your dates fixed I'll call Madame Bialgues and tell her to get the apartment ready.'

'I'll give you plenty of warning,' she said. 'And guess what, they're flying me back on Concorde!'

'And so they should,' he said staunchly. 'I'm missing you.'

Her voice caressed him. 'What are you doing with yourself?'

'Not a lot. To tell you the truth, I'm bored. Lauterbach's coming over later.' He was grateful that she couldn't see his eyes.

'Well, behave yourselves,' she said. 'And when you put your head on the pillow tonight, remember I love you.'

He relinquished the receiver reluctantly and opened the writing-bureau. The folder with Lambert's sheets of typescript lay on the blotting-pad. He placed Armstrong's address-book and the fake warrant-card beside it with the tape of Lucy's message.

He was slotting a J. J. Cale tape in the deck when Lauterbach came through the door, spruce in a pink shirt, jeans and buckled loafers.

He threw himself down on the sofa and stretched. 'You gonna buy me a beer?'

Raven uncapped two bottles of Labatt and put one on the table in front of his friend. 'You were brilliant. I don't know what the hell I'd have done without you.'

Lauterbach tilted the bottle and swallowed. 'I was on

the right end of a gun for a change. Know something, we make a good team. We'd have left those Latinos for dead if I'd had you in Medellin.'

'I spoke to Mallory,' said Raven. 'He's adamant. Nick never even looked at the file. He was just doing his friend Mallory a favour.'

Lauterbach took another swig from the bottle. 'What did *Mallory* think he was getting?'

'Something that'd help him find his girlfriend. That's what Lucy told him anyway and he wanted to believe her.'

Lauterbach pulled a face. 'She sounds like a real sweet lady. Supplies the keys and some bullshit information and sits there popping gum while the house goes up in flames?'

'I know what you mean,' said Raven. 'But you've got to get these things in perspective. You've got Lambert who's had his wicked way with her and dumped her. Just another piece on the side. He couldn't have realized that she was simply biding her time. Jealousy's a very powerful emotion. Then his safe gets robbed and the penny drops. All he wants is his property back.'

Lauterbach pounded the cushions and stretched out his legs. 'And you think he knows where Lucy is?'

'I'm sure of it,' said Raven. 'He'll be in Hollywood Mews tomorrow. I've got a surprise waiting for him.'

'Uhuh,' said Lauterbach. 'That's something you've always got plenty of. And what about me? Do I tag along too?'

Raven moved his head regretfully. 'Not on this occasion. It's got to be one on one.'

Lauterbach sighed. 'You're still not taking me seriously, are you?'

'Oh but I am,' Raven answered, dragging the phone across the table. He dialled Jerry Soo's home number.

'It's me,' he announced. 'That guy you know on the Surrey force. What was his name again?'

'Dick Fowler?'

'What's his rank?'

'Assistant-Commissioner in charge of CID.'

'Do you trust him?'

Soo's tone grew starchy. 'What are you driving at here? Dick's got more time in than I have and there's never been a whisper against him. You're talking about the Surrey constabulary not the Met. Anything Fowler does is done by the book. Why wouldn't I trust him?'

Raven wrapped himself in his shoulders and gave his words emphasis. 'I want you to get hold of him. You know, sound him out. Say you have this friend who's got evidence of a criminal conspiracy taking place on his patch. Tell him when the time's right I'll supply the names, places and evidence. Tell him who I am if you like. I don't give a shit. Just as long as he understands that I'm serious.'

Soo's voice was aghast. 'Are you out of your mind, for God's sake? The man's a senior police officer with a reputation at stake. He'll want to know a lot more than that before he commits himself.'

'Then give me the chance to talk to him,' Raven argued.

The line was quiet for a moment. Then Soo spoke again. 'Is there anyone else involved with you in this business?'

Raven kept his eyes on Lauterbach. 'My neighbour. You met him at Christmas time, an American. There's no problem there. He's as solid as a rock.'

'And that's all you're going to tell me?'

'It's all I *can* tell you right now.'

'Do you know what you're doing?' Soo asked quietly.

'No,' said Raven. 'But I'm still going to do it. I'm offering the chance every cop dreams about. The big one. And it's there for the taking. All I want you to do is set up the meeting. Is that asking too much of you?'

'I'll have a word with him and get back to you. I won't say anything about your neighbour for the moment. What's happening with Kirstie?'

'She's in New York. She'll be back at the end of next week so don't let me down, Jerry.'

'I'll give it my best shot and let you know. And take care of yourself.'

Lauterbach appeared to have taken the conversation in his stride with his eyes closed as though hearing a fife-and-drum band in the distance. He opened his eyes and drew a rolled-up joint from his shirt pocket and lit it. They listened to J. J. Cale's husky voice, passing the joint to and fro, ' "As solid as a rock",' quoted Lauterbach approvingly. 'That's not a bad thing to have on your headstone!'

Raven looked at him smiling. 'I know something else to put. "He never grew up", for instance.'

Lauterbach thumbed his smoke into the ashtray. 'I grew up the same way as you did, believing in the same sort of things. It never kept me out of mischief but it sure opened my eyes to the facts of life.'

'You're my ace in the hole,' said Raven.

Lauterbach winked. 'You want to get stoned, make a night of it?'

Raven felt the room crowding in on him. 'We're both going to need clear heads in the morning. You'll know soon enough what's happening.'

'Cool,' said Lauterbach, swinging his feet to the floor. 'Just yell when you need me.'

Raven unfastened the door to the deck. The wind blowing off the river held the soft promise of rain. He watched Lauterbach as far as the end of the gangway and bolted the door. Then he filled the bath and lowered his long body into the hot scented water. The vein on his left leg showed no swelling. He leaned back and thought about Lauterbach.

He was the only child of a wealthy Monterey widower with little interest in his son. Lauterbach had attended a series of boarding-schools in various parts of the state, running away when he felt like it, being twice expelled. He was finally placed in a gung-ho military academy with a reputation for turning goats into lambs: a record tarnished by Lauterbach's short tour of duty. He left home at the age of twenty with a cheque for fifty thousand dollars and his father's firmly expressed wish that this

would be the last time they met. His next stop was
Colombia where he had a short dalliance with a Medellin
drugs dealer. The arrangement concluded with Lauterbach leaving the country at speed for Paraguay. His
money had grown to three hundred thousand dollars. He
visited the US Embassy and reported his passport as
stolen. The replacement document bore no sign of his
stay in Colombia. He took the next Varig flight for
London and had stayed there since. Raven knew him as
a maverick with an ingrained dislike of authority and the
ferocity of a lion when crossed. It was a combination of
attitudes that Raven found heady at times. Above all,
he admired Lauterbach's insouciance when faced with
danger.

Raven pulled on his pyjamas and crawled under the
duvet. His last conscious thought was of Kirstie.

Chapter Eight

Raven opened his eyes just after seven o'clock. The first thing they lit upon was the cheese sandwich he had taken to bed and forgotten. It lay with the cut-glass bottles and silver-backed brushes on the dressing-table, an offence to Kirstie's dainty femininity. He had shed his pyjamas during the night and the bath-sheet had been left on the floor. He put on his robe and threw the sandwich through the window. It was still dark outside and the neighbouring boats were wrapped in the weekend torpor. It was Sunday, with no post or newspaper delivery. He made himself coffee and took the mug back to bed with him. It was peaceful to lie there with the light out. He must have dozed off.

It was gone nine o'clock when he turned the radio on. The weather report forecast rain. He stayed where he was for a while, buoyed by controlled excitement. With Lambert in his sights he had little concern for Mallory or Lucy. Lambert remained an enigma. Like all skilled liars he was able to bring credence to his falsehoods; a chess-player able to envisage the gambits left open for his opponent and move accordingly.

Raven made his bed, tidied the room and shaved. He took his chalk-line blue flannel suit from the closet and selected a button-down white shirt and a grey tie. His Burberry and a Bates weatherproof cap completed his outfit. He put his keys and change in his pocket, his note-case snug on his hip. He considered his stiffly held fingers.

They were steady enough. Lambert took note of such things. Raven unlocked the Orion and drove through empty streets pursued by the melancholy of church bells. He found a place to park behind Elm Park Mansions. Mallory's car was still slumped on its wheel-rims. Raven used his keys to gain access to the building and mounted the stairs.

Mallory's neighbour was waiting outside her door, an elderly woman in a housecoat and slippers. There was a smell of burned toast in the corridor. She looked at him suspiciously.

Raven raised his cap, showing her the keys in his other hand. 'Martin's away for a couple of days. I'm keeping an eye on his flat,' he explained.

She bridled. 'His phone was ringing long after midnight. The noise stopped me going to sleep. He gives no thought at all to other people, no consideration. It's just not good enough, you know.'

He sought to bring reason to bear. 'I don't see how you can hold Martin responsible but I'll certainly tell him.'

'You'd better,' she snapped. 'Can't you turn the phone off or something?'

'I'm afraid not,' he answered. 'He's got an answering-machine.'

She lifted a monitory finger. 'Well, you can tell him this when you see him – I intend making a complaint to the Residents' Association about his behaviour. It's disgraceful.'

She slammed her door shut.

He unlocked Mallory's flat. The sitting-room was frowsty, the air still denuded of oxygen. He lowered a window and activated the answering-machine. A familiar voice spoke after the tone.

'It's Ludovic Lambert, Martin. This is in case you haven't heard from Mister Pinner. I'm completely distraught and I need to talk to you urgently. I'm at Hollywood Mews until Tuesday. Please call me here. It's important.'

Raven put the tape in his raincoat pocket and went into the bedroom. There was no sign that an interloper had visited the premises. He relocked the front door and descended the stairs to the street. The first drops of rain were falling. He hurried along the Fulham Road. Neptune's Sea-Food Kitchen was one of the few restaurants in the neighbourhood that served Sunday lunch. He sat near the window and ordered a dozen Whitstable oysters and a glass of house champagne. He laced each mollusc with Tabasco and ate, watching the pub across the street. Raven knew it as the first and last port of call for those in need of an alcoholic crutch, the refuge for determined drinkers. A sad lonely place to be on a wet Sunday morning with nothing but memories, perceived and imagined. The thought, like the sound of the church bells, depressed Raven. He called for his bill.

It was raining hard by the time he left, slanting stair-rods driving in relentlessly from the west. He pulled his cap down and hid his neck with his collar. He walked past the cinema on the corner and turned left towards Hollywood Close. Lambert's mud-spattered Bentley was parked outside a bright yellow door fitted with two new locks. There were three windows on the upper floor, two on the lower. Lights shone in all of them.

He pressed the bell. Lambert opened the door, elegant in a tan cashmere jacket, dark-brown slacks and brogue shoes with leather laces. His face showed surprise. He glanced over Raven's shoulder.

'I'm alone,' said Raven.

'Well, come on in!' Lambert said quickly.

Raven wiped his feet on the mat and closed the door. There was a briefcase on the table under the gilt-framed mirror. Raven had a sense of *déjà vu* gained from Mallory's description.

'Let me take your coat,' offered Lambert.

Raven's fingers closed on the tape in his pocket. 'I think I'll keep it on for the moment.'

Lambert tapped a thermometer on the wall and

frowned. 'It *is* cold in here. I leave the heating off when I'm in the country and the house takes a while to warm up. We had a burglary and I had to get rid of the cleaner.'

He opened the door to the sitting-room. Picture-lamps illuminated a Skeaping print of the Camargue and a display-case showing a collection of antique musical boxes. A life-size bronze cat glowered from the carpet. The windows were hung with grey silk curtains. A couple of comfortable armchairs were positioned one each side of the low teak table.

Raven unbuckled the belt of his Burberry and sat with his back to the hallway.

Lambert opened a cabinet. A light shone on an array of bottles and glasses. 'What can I get you to drink?' he said.

'Nothing,' said Raven.

Lambert poured brandy into a balloon glass and sat, warming the glass in his palms. His eyes showed no more than hospitable interest. 'So what news do you have of Martin?'

Raven tapped a cigarette from the blue pack and took his time lighting it.

'I'm not going to beat about the bush. It's too late for the social niceties. Martin came to me a week or so ago in a state of distress. He told me about a girl he had fallen in love with, a Chinese student of his at the Wycherly. He said that she had suddenly vanished without leaving a word of explanation. It was the rest of his story I found hard to credit. I imagine you know what I'm talking about?'

Lambert's knuckles blanched as he tightened his grip on his glass. His tone of voice was unchanged.

'Did he tell you that he got one of his prison acquaintances to break into my safe? That he suborned my secretary?'

'He told me *everything*,' Raven emphasized. 'Including the fact that you didn't inform the police about your safe being robbed.'

'I find your manner extremely offensive,' said Lambert. 'Are you giving that as the reason for that masquerade you staged down at Corton Bassett? What are you – some sort of professional snooper, Mister Pinner?'

'Just a friend of Martin's,' said Raven, dribbling smoke from his nostrils. 'Trying to get him out of this mess that he's in.'

Lambert's hands were steady again. 'Do you condone blackmail?'

It was the word Raven had been waiting to hear. 'Martin's a fool,' he said, 'but he isn't a blackmailer. It's just not his style.'

Lambert refilled his glass from the bottle in front of him. 'You've only heard one side of the story. The least you can do is listen to mine before you start sitting in judgement.'

Raven swung one leg over the other. 'Why not? It's what I'm here for.'

Lambert was not bereft of imagination. His explanation might be flawed but his brain would be working.

Lambert put his glass down and stood with his back to the window. 'It all seems like some terrible nightmare. I know it sounds trite but it's true. I had a phone call two nights after the robbery. I didn't recognize the voice but the accent was cockney. He said that the man who burgled my safe had been drowned. He said he knew where my property was.'

He paused for effect like a Shakespearian actor before bringing tidings of tragedy.

'If I wanted my property back it would cost me two hundred thousand pounds.'

Raven looked suitably impressed. 'That's a lot of money even in these days.'

'He said if I didn't produce it he'd go to the tabloids. I tried to explain that I didn't *have* two hundred thousand pounds or anything like it. I told him that this house belonged to the Foundation but he refused to believe me.

111

According to him, a man in my position always has access to funds. There was no one I could turn to for help. Not a soul in the world. Do you see the dilemma I was in?'

Raven frowned. 'I might do if I knew what was in the file.'

Lambert pondered as rain lashed the window panes. Then he shrugged, giving the most distant of smiles. 'What's the difference. You seem to know everything else. The facts are simple enough. The Wycherly's no different from any other similar organization. There are certain aspects of our business affairs that have to be dealt with in confidence. That's why the papers were encoded. Why I typed them myself. Lucy Ashton knew I was meeting a German colleague in London. She also knew that I was taking the file with me. Her mistake was in assuming that this had something to do with students who'd been transferred to one of our other branches. She couldn't have been further from the truth.'

He paused for a while, shaking his head.

'Some of our donors wished to remain anonymous and I respected their wishes. That file contained their names and the amounts of their gifts. The irony is that this information is totally useless to anyone else, including the Inland Revenue. But you can imagine what a muckraking reporter could do with it. The Charity Commissioners have unlimited powers of investigation. If something like this were brought to their attention, it would mean the end of the Foundation.'

Raven fingered the knot in his tie. 'And you think that Martin is part of this blackmail attempt – is that what you're saying?'

'What would *you* think?' argued Lambert. 'I knew that my safe had been robbed. And I knew that Martin and Lucy were responsible. Then Lucy takes off and I was getting these strange calls from Martin trying to get hold of her. It was logical to believe that they were both at the heart of this latest outrage.'

His voice and manner were right. The avowal of guilt. But an inner certainty told Raven that Lambert was lying.

'Let's get something straight,' said Raven. 'I don't give a fuck about your tax-dodging antics. But if you *do* go down, you'll take Martin with you. I don't intend to let that happen.'

Lambert resumed his place at the table. 'Why didn't he come to me in the first place? Make a clean breast of things. We could have worked something out together.'

'He was frightened,' said Raven. 'People in that sort of situation don't always reason. They panic. Martin's no criminal. He had a job that he liked. No financial difficulties. He was a man who enjoyed life. His only mistake was falling in love.'

'Love?' Lambert said sarcastically. 'The girl was just amusing herself.'

'The point is that Martin doesn't know where the file is. Nick Berry kept it. Now Lucy's skedaddled, leaving Martin to face the music.'

Lambert looked up from his glass. 'Where is he now? Why won't he talk to me?'

'He's leaving the talking to me,' said Raven. 'But we don't seem to be making much progress. You tell me you're being blackmailed. You're a highly intelligent man but you're out of your depth. You're dealing with scoundrels of the worst possible kind. I've *seen* the damage that blackmail can cause. I wouldn't wish it on my worst enemy.'

Lambert looked shocked. 'Is that how you view me – as an enemy?'

'I'm your unwilling ally,' said Raven. 'Suppose I could get your papers back without paying a single penny? Would you be prepared to sign an affidavit absolving Martin of any part in the robbery?'

'Of course,' Lambert said quickly. 'How could you do it?'

'By using my knowledge of human behaviour. I'll tell

you a true story, Mister Lambert. I knew a schoolmaster once. Happily married with a child but a homosexual. He went through the same sort of experience as you. Demands for money with the threat of disclosure. They bled him dry. He was too ashamed to go to the police. So he waited until his wife had taken his daughter to school and blew his brains out. That taught me a lesson. There's only one way of dealing with a blackmailer. You outsmart him. Use stupidity to work in your favour.'

'I couldn't do it,' said Lambert. 'I wouldn't be able to carry it off.'

'I'm talking about me, not you,' Raven said. 'How do you get in touch with these people?'

'They've been calling me every night at the Wycherly. It's always the same voice. Threatening. Reminding me that I've got two weeks to find the money.'

'Do they know you're in London?'

'I had to tell them. The man said he'd be calling tonight.'

'Do you know when?'

'About eight o'clock.'

'Right,' said Raven. 'Then here's what you do. Tell him that a friend is ready to lend you the money for your property.'

'Why would he trust you?'

'Greed,' said Raven. 'The prospect of two hundred thousand pounds exerts a strong hold on the imagination. Tell him your friend doesn't want to reveal his name at this juncture but he'll keep any appointment that's made. In the mean time I'll have the affidavit drawn up. It's Martin I'm doing this for, not you.'

'How do I reach you? At your Floral Street number?'

'I never lived there,' said Raven. He accompanied Lambert into the hallway and donned his cap. 'I'll talk to you later.'

Lambert summoned his last shreds of dignity. 'I'm not an ungrateful man, Mister Pinner. If you get my property back, I'll prove it.'

'All you've got to do is sign the affidavit,' said Raven. He ducked into the rain and hastened back to his car.

It was a typical wet Sunday evening with little traffic along the Embankment. The houseboats nosed one another on the swollen river. A light shone in Lauterbach's cabin. Raven let himself into the sitting-room and heard the familiar wash of bilge in the hold. He hung his coat and cap in the corridor and checked his answering-machine. There was a message from Jerry Soo asking him to call. Soo's voice answered immediately. 'I managed to get hold of Fowler. It was heavy going at first but he listened. I told him I'd known you for twenty-five years, that you were a man of your word. Anyway, he's agreed to meet you. I'm picking him up on my way from the baths in the morning. We should be with you about ten.'

Raven's neck muscles tightened. 'What do you think the prospects are, Jerry?'

'He wouldn't be coming to see you if he wasn't interested,' said Soo. 'You'll have to talk to him yourself. And I warn you, he isn't a fool.'

Raven sat in his chair, contemplating the snapshot of Kirstie on the writing-bureau. He had taken it on their honeymoon in Martinique and it showed her clad in a topless bikini clinging to a sign on a dinghy that read DÉFENSE À BORDER. He remembered the injunction wryly. They'd been living together for five years by then, each aware of the need for personal freedom, rejecting the lure of 'togetherness' in favour of what had become a caring sexual comradeship. Marriage had been no more than an affirmation of mutual trust. Kirstie still feared what she dubbed Raven's 'Captain Midnight' ventures, pointing out that what she needed was a warm, loving companion not an ex-cop with personality problems. Why didn't he put it all down on paper, she suggested, and get it out of his system that way? He'd bought a personal computer and written two pages before accepting his total lack of talent.

He waited until ten past eight and called Lambert at

Hollywood Mews. The line was engaged. He gave it another few minutes and tried again. This time the phone was picked up.

'It's Pinner,' said Raven. 'What happened?'

'He said there was no way he was going to show himself in London but he gave me an address in Hindhead. Do you want it or not?'

Raven pulled the scribble-pad across the table. 'Go ahead.'

'The Old Rectory, Grayshott Road. He says you turn off at the petrol-station after the junction to Haslemere. You'll see a lane on the right. That's where the house is. He wants you to be there at seven o'clock on Wednesday night. Alone. He's phoning me back for your answer.'

'Tell him I'll be there. I'll let you know what happens,' said Raven.

He called Directory Enquiries, giving the address in front of him. A recorded voice said, 'The number you require is 0428 735500.'

It was the same number that Armstrong had called from his flat. Raven spoke to Lauterbach. 'You'd better get yourself over here.'

'I'll be there in five,' said Lauterbach.

Raven left the deck-door ajar and took a bottle of Bell's and a couple of shot-glasses from the drinks cupboard, ice and Malvern water from the kitchen. Lauterbach ambled in seconds later, wearing the UCLA sweatshirt, cords and his usual Sunday stubble. He shook the rain from his shoulders and sank on the couch.

'Don't tell me,' he said, polishing his spectacles. 'You gonna lay some horrendous shit on me. It's written all over your face!'

Raven poured three fingers of Scotch in each glass and pushed the ice bucket in Lauterbach's direction. His own drink he diluted with water.

'There are a couple of things I want to talk about. The first is, I'm forty-eight years old with all the money I need

116

to see me through however long's left. I've realized that none of that would mean a thing without Kirstie. I've known that ever since the day I met her. I made a decision last night after talking to her. She deserves a helluva lot more than she's getting from me.'

Lauterbach poked a finger at the ice in his glass. 'I've heard you say the same sort of thing fifty times. What happened with Lambert?'

No writer, Raven still had a good feeling for narrative. He took Lauterbach through the scene in Hollywood Mews.

Lauterbach listened in silence, sipping his Scotch.

He sat up a little straighter when Raven had finished. 'Do you really believe that he went for that bullshit, for crissakes! It's a trap. He thinks you know where his papers are.'

'I'm counting on it,' Raven said. 'I've got a feeling Armstrong and his brother-in-law will be only too glad to refresh my memory.'

'Then fuck it,' said Lauterbach. 'Don't even go near the place. A guy wants to know where the rattler is before he goes looking for kindling wood.'

'Hollywood Mews,' said Raven. 'That's where the rattler is. I'll tell you how I think this went. Lambert came back and found that his safe had been robbed. He was the only one who knew the importance of his loss. But he didn't panic. He goes through the charade of telling the police that the safe was empty but his brain's already working. Whoever robbed him had the keys. He decides that Lucy's responsible. So he gets hold of Armstrong and his brother-in-law. They turn up at Lucy's posing as cops and keep her holed-up somewhere safe. Then Lambert turns up and Lucy starts talking. She tips in Mallory and gives them Nick Berry's name. Armstrong and Terry pay Nick a visit. He tells them the truth. He did what he did as a favour and gave the papers to Mallory.'

Lauterbach lifted his head. 'And that's the last anyone

sees of Nick Berry. You think they killed him?'

'I don't know,' said Raven. 'All we've got is the Coroner's verdict. But I've got a shrewd idea what happened next. Armstrong and Terry decide they're sitting on a gold-mine. All they need is the missing papers and they can bleed Lambert dry.'

Lauterbach frowned. 'And you're saying Lambert doesn't know what they're up to?'

'I'm sure he does,' Raven replied with conviction. 'He's smart and he's devious. He can run rings round them. But he still needs his property back. He's gambling that I'm going to lead him to it. OK?'

'I guess so,' said Lauterbach.

'Good,' said Raven. 'Let's get back to the business in hand.'

Raven rummaged through his collection of road-atlases until he found a linen-backed Ordnance Survey map featuring the area around Hindhead. He placed the map on the table between them and checked the details. The house was clearly marked at the end of a drive and surrounded by trees on three sides. There was a church a short distance away. Other than that there was nothing between the garage and the village a mile further west. Raven closed the map and settled back in his chair.

'They're expecting me to show up on Wednesday, right? But we're going there tomorrow night. Take a close look at the place. A sort of rehearsal. It'll be dark so we shouldn't have problems. Do you like the idea or not?'

Lauterbach nodded indifferently. 'Any more news from your friend Jerry?'

'He's bringing someone to see me in the morning.' Raven jerked his thumb at the writing-bureau. 'They can see the evidence for themselves.'

Lauterbach sauntered across the room to the fruit bowl. He chose a sharp knife and came back paring an apple, his forehead tight with concentration. He deposited the ring of peel in the waste-paper basket and spoke through a mouthful of Golden Delicious.

'Have you got any idea what a stun-gun is?'

Raven goggled. 'A stun-gun! I remember an article in *Science* a year or so ago. It's an American invention, a device about the size of a large torch. It's got this transformer that boosts the charge from a handful of batteries into forty thousand volts or more. The SAS has them. Otherwise they're illegal. People are said to have died from heart attacks.'

Lauterbach sent the apple core after the peel and wiped his lips. 'They're standard equipment in some states back home. The police use them for crowd control. Nobody's died from a heart attack that I ever heard of. All they do is lay the guy out for twenty minutes. Then he comes round and wonders what happened.'

Raven spoke with a feeling of apprehension. 'How come you're such an expert?'

'I've got one,' Lauterbach said blandly.

Raven's glass clattered down on the table. 'Where?' he demanded.

Lauterbach was totally relaxed. 'In Amanda's garage.'

'That's beautiful,' said Raven, wagging his head. 'A girl working in the Foreign Office with a lethal weapon stashed in her garage. You've got to be out of your mind. Where the hell did you get it?'

'I bought it from a guy who came into the shop. I've been taking it down to the country and practising. There's nothing I've hit that didn't walk or fly away after a little rest. It's just the sort of thing to have in an emergency.'

Raven smiled in spite of himself. 'Don't bring it anywhere near me. We're going to do this with guile not guns.'

Lauterbach came to his feet. 'That was a good apple. Let me know what happens in the morning with Jerry.'

Chapter Nine

One of the first things Raven did on Monday morning was call Mrs Burrows and postpone her ministrations until later that day. He had no preconceived ideas about the man Jerry Soo was bringing but he knew the importance of creating a favourable image. With this on his mind he donned a Lillywhite fishing-sweater over black corduroy trousers and stout country shoes. He brushed his hair carefully and applied a touch of Kirstie's lightest sprays. A serious man, he decided, turning away from the mirror. A man who both gave and demanded respect.

It was just after nine thirty and Soo would be punctual. Raven busied himself in the kitchen, setting his aunt's silver tray with breakfast cups, sugar and cream. He added the jar of powdered chocolate. Soo liked to flavour his coffee. The percolator was already rumbling. Jerry held a season ticket to the pool at Imperial College. He swam thirty lengths every morning wearing an old-fashioned bathing-costume and waterproof goggles. He was a karate dan, an errant Buddhist, incapable of putting an injured animal out of its misery, and Raven had a deep and abiding affection for him.

Raven heard the unmistakable sound of Soo's arrival and carried the tray into the sitting-room. He released the door at the foot of the steps and stood by the window. Soo was the first to appear on deck, bouncing along on the balls of his feet. He was wearing a raincoat like a cloak over a neat, dark business-suit. Raven's immediate

120

impression of the man with him was of bulk. He carried it effortlessly, distributing his weight on massive legs with elephantine precision. Raven shut the door behind them.

Soo made the introductions. 'Commander Fowler, John Raven.'

Fowler offered his hand. He was in his early fifties with grizzled hair, a thick neck and inquisitive eyes. He had on a brown three-piece tweed suit with a gold chain and fob stretched across his waistcoat. He lowered his considerable weight on the sofa next to Soo and turned his gaze on the snapshot of Kirstie.

'My wife,' explained Raven, lifting the percolator. 'Do you take cream and sugar, Commander?'

'Black, please, no sugar,' Fowler responded. He raised the cup to his lips. His fingernails were impeccable.

'It's good of you to come to see me,' said Raven. He had spoken to Soo after Lauterbach had left, telling him about his confrontation with Lambert, his visit to Armstrong. 'I take it you've heard what happened yesterday?'

'Indeed,' said Fowler. His West Country burr gave his voice a hint of reticence. 'Jerry showed me your service record. To be frank, I found it alarming.'

'I can imagine,' said Raven. 'I wasn't exactly popular.'

Fowler nodded amiably. 'You're described as disruptive. A man who's prepared to cut corners in order to secure a conviction.'

It was twelve years ago but the memory still evoked resentment. 'I'll tell you what I did,' said Raven. 'I reported a crooked cop for taking bribes from criminals. That resulted in me being hauled in front of a Disciplinary Board and suspended from duty. I had to do the rest myself. But I put him behind bars where he belonged and resigned. Is that what you'd call disruptive?'

'I'm just repeating what I read,' Fowler said peaceably. 'The point is, you're bringing serious allegations against someone who, as far as we know, has an unblemished record. What we need is evidence.'

Raven forced himself to be patient. He opened the writing-bureau and placed the file, Armstrong's address-book, the false warrant-card and the two tapes from Mallory's answering-machine on the table. Each article was given its provenance. He seemed to be set apart in that moment, seeking Fowler's approval and understanding. Raven continued quietly, respectfully even. 'You're here because Jerry's vouched for you. And you're the only one I can think of in a position to help me.' He swept the things on the table into a large manuscript-size envelope and laid it in front of Fowler. 'Take it,' he urged, 'study it. Ask any questions you like as long as I know where I stand.'

The Commander's eyes lifted from the envelope to Raven.

'What sort of help are you asking for?'

There was something about Fowler's manner that inspired Raven's confidence. He had a sense of being in the presence of a man who'd go the second mile with you and carry you the rest of the way if it proved to be necessary.

'You've been frank with me,' said Raven. 'I'll be the same with you. I don't think you understand the sort of man that we're dealing with. Lambert's a wily scoundrel on the brink of disaster. If he gets even the faintest inkling that the police are involved, we'll lose him. We're not talking about some petty false-pretences. This is a man with access to money and the right sort of contacts. The last thing he'll do is just sit there and wait. I know this may sound presumptuous but I've got to impose some conditions.'

Fowler put his cup down, frowning. 'You mean *suggestions*,' he corrected.

'Whatever,' said Raven. 'I need an undertaking that you won't make a move on Lambert without letting me know. And I want my phone left alone and nobody on my tail. And finally, your assurance that my name won't appear in any of the records. In other words, no publicity.'

Soo turned to Fowler quickly. 'John's worried about his wife finding out. She's dead set against this sort of thing.'

'If this case ever does come to court,' said Fowler, 'there are plenty of ways we can protect your identity, but you'd still have to make a statement. And the prosecution service will have to be apprised of the facts.'

'We're quibbling,' answered Raven. 'I'm giving you more than a statement. I'm giving you hard facts and bodies. All I'm asking for in return is to be sure of the capture.'

A note of wry scepticism crept into Fowler's reply. 'You seem to be taking a lot for granted. I mean, I can't give up experienced officers while this thing drags on for weeks – even months. We just don't have the resources.'

The objection was a reminder of Kirstie's impending return. 'Ten days,' he told Fowler. 'If I haven't delivered Lambert by then, you can make your own arrangements.'

Fowler took the manuscript envelope in his hands. 'And this?'

'It's yours,' said Raven. 'Evidence. Whatever happens, evidence is what you're going to need.'

Fowler fingered the fob on his watch-chain. 'Do you mind if Jerry and I have a word in private?'

Raven took the tray into the kitchen and closed the door. It was impossible to hear more than the muffled sound of conversation. He sat, staring at the phone on the dresser. Maybe this was what the Fate Sisters had been holding in store for him. A reminder that even the instructed were better off never achieving more than a glimpse of their final triumph. He shrugged. Ah well, Martinique was no more than a five-hour flight from Paris.

Soo opened the kitchen door. Raven accompanied him into the sitting-room. Fowler spoke in his slow amiable voice.

'This is what I'm prepared to do. You've got ten days free from interference during which time I'll go through

123

this stuff that you've given me. I'll be in close touch with Jerry and this number will reach me night or day.'

He pushed a slip of paper across the table and lumbered to his feet, smiling. 'It's a pity you never joined the Surrey constabulary. You might still be a copper.'

As he and Jerry left, he turned from the door at the foot of the steps and waved. Raven lifted a hand in reply, his confidence hammered back in place. He was unburdened. Gone was the need to dignify his actions with moral persuasion.

He pushed his arms through the sleeves of his Burberry and strode out on deck. Lauterbach was squatting outside his cabin adjusting his television aerial. He jumped down as Raven approached. 'Hi! You look pleased with yourself. I saw them leave. What happened?'

Raven sat on the bunk. Fresh air blew through the open porthole. The floor had been swept, order restored in the kitchen and sleeping-quarters. 'Fowler's OK,' said Raven. 'I've got a phone number that'll reach him at any time and ten days to wrap things up. He's a man I can trust.'

Lauterbach leaned a shoulder against the bulkhead. 'Does he know about Wednesday?'

'I told him,' said Raven. 'Let's talk about tonight. The idea's to get a close look at the house, check who's living there. And make sure they don't see us.'

Lauterbach grinned lopsidedly. 'You're looking at the guy Miss Peabody called the best tracker in the entire troop of Cubs!'

'Terrific,' Raven said drily. 'Let's hope the years haven't dimmed your abilities. Lambert's already seen the Orion at Corton Bassett so I'm renting a car. Have you got any dark clothes you can wear?'

Lauterbach pulled a dark-green loden coat out of a cupboard. 'I've got a pair of dark pants and some black sneakers. What time do you want to take off? I've got to open the store at some point. There's a woman coming in to look at some brass.'

'I'll see you on the boat at five thirty,' said Raven. 'It'll give us time to cover any last-minute thoughts for tonight. And wear your dark clothes.'

He sauntered up to the King's Road. Turner's Budget Hire offered a selection of low-mileage vehicles for rental. Raven decided on a black four-door Honda. He made sure that there was plenty of room behind the steering-wheel and produced his driving-licence and a credit card. He signed a seven-day agreement and insurance form and waited until the petrol, oil and tyre pressures had been checked.

It was twenty past five when he parked under the trees on the pub forecourt. Mrs Burrows had left the sitting-room bright and welcoming, the silver polished, the much-darned Aubusson carefully positioned between the glass-topped table and the two sofas. There was a message from Jerry Soo on the answering-machine.

'I thought you might like to know that you made a good impression on Fowler. He's a good man, John, so don't blow it. And stay in touch.'

Raven left the door to the deck ajar and unfastened the deep closet where Kirstie kept her cameras. He took the aluminium-framed night-glasses from their case. A light intensifier increased the clarity of vision. He put the glasses and his torch in his raincoat pocket and spread the map out on the table. He measured the length of the drive against the inch-to-mile scale. He made it somewhat less than two hundred yards from Grayshott Road to the symbol representing the Old Rectory. Trees crowded in on three sides of the house and turning-circle. A cross marked the church a quarter of a mile west along Gray-shott Road. It was vital to find somewhere to leave the car out of sight.

Lauterbach breezed in, wearing the loden coat and the black trainers. He sat down on the sofa next to Raven, his face showing no more than mild curiosity.

Raven refolded the map and gave it to Lauterbach. 'You can do the navigating. Here's the scenario. We'll find a safe place to park where the car won't be seen. Then we separate. You'll take the back of the house, I'll take the front. We need to know exactly what's going on inside, remember. How many people are in there, if there's a dog, for instance. Anything that'll help us on Wednesday.'

Lauterbach pushed the map in his pocket, smiling. 'I told you, Miss Peabody taught me all the old Indian tricks.'

'There'll be no way of communicating once we've split,' said Raven. 'We'll have to check back at base every half-hour. Base is wherever we leave the car. We'll try the church first. If one of us doesn't show, the other one waits until he knows what's happened. OK?'

Lauterbach nodded. 'A good tracker's always prepared. It's part of his training.'

'A good tracker doesn't smoke dope,' Raven said drily.

Lauterbach's face sobered. 'Why don't you loosen up for crissakes. What happened to your sense of humour?'

'I'm sorry,' said Raven, 'but it isn't the time for joking. This is serious business. And if we should get a pull on the way, we're looking for the Frensham Ponds Hotel. It's a few miles the other side of Hindhead.'

'Got it,' said Lauterbach.

They climbed the steps and walked across to the Honda, Lauterbach inspected the tyres and settled himself in the passenger seat.

They reached the wide sweep round the Devil's Punch-bowl fifty minutes later. A restaurant blazed on the corner of the turn-off to Haslemere. The map lay open in Lauterbach's lap.

'Slow down,' he instructed. 'The filling-station's coming up any moment now.'

The office and pumps were closed. Raven pulled the Honda on to Grayshott Road, slackening his speed as they passed the lane to the Old Rectory. The church loomed on their right. He drove through the open gate and stopped. The headlamps stared at the notice pinned to the door:

THIS CHURCH IS CLOSED. ALL ENQUIRIES SHOULD BE MADE TO SAINT MARK'S CHURCH IN HINDHEAD.

There was no traffic in either direction. Raven killed the lights and the engine. 'This'll do us,' he said, looking down at his watch. 'I make it seven nineteen precisely.'

Lauterbach turned his wrist and nodded. 'I'll see you back here in thirty minutes, OK?'

He pulled up his coat-collar and sauntered off towards the lane swinging the Great Dane's lead in his hand, a man out for an evening stroll with his dog.

Raven left the car unlocked and walked round the back of the church. A paved path led past untended gravestones to a barbed-wire fence at the end of the burial-ground. He gauged his position. The house lay beyond the trees in front of him. He placed gloved hands on the post supporting the five strands of barbed-wire and felt it give slightly under his weight. He rocked the post in both directions, increasing the pressure until the pole slumped at an angle. He lifted it free of the hole and laid it down gently. Then he raised the skirts of his rain-coat and stepped over the tangle of wire.

He stood stock-still, eyes and ears alert to any hint of danger. A pattern of sound established itself in the eerie gloom of the massive trees: a whisper of wind in the upper branches, the hoot of an owl in the distance. He moved forward, lifting his feet high as creepers rooted deep in the mulched leaves dragged at his ankles. He kept his eyes on the faint glow of light at the end of the driveway, using each tree as cover until he stood on the edge of the turning-circle. The Old Rectory was no more than twenty yards away, a three-storey Victorian building with a lamp burning in the porch. He panned his night-glasses, dragging the front of the gloomy house into focus. The windows on the ground floor were shuttered, the ones above unlit but curtained. A curl of smoke drifted from a chimney. Otherwise the house looked deserted. He put the glasses back in his pocket, leaving his hands free. His rubber-soled shoes were noiseless as he crept forward, bending low in front of the shuttered windows. A telephone rang inside the house. He heard a man shout. Someone extinguished the lamp in the porch. The phone continued to ring unanswered. The house fell silent once more.

Raven ran for the trees, sure now that his hunch had been well founded. He made his way back to the churchyard and lifted the fence back in position. Lauterbach was waiting in the car, the radio playing softly. Raven climbed in beside him and silenced the music.

'Well, don't just sit there grinning,' he said. 'I want to know what happened.'

Lauterbach popped a stick of gum in his mouth and took his time to answer. 'I'll tell you,' he said. 'There's a yard at the back of the house with a garage and some kind of room over it. I was no more than twenty feet away from the kitchen window. There were two guys playing cards at the table. And guess what – Armstrong was one of them.'

'What did the other one look like?'

Lauterbach shifted his gum. 'Older than Armstrong with brown curly hair. They hadn't even bothered to pull the shades. I could see them clearly.'

'Did you hear the phone ring?' asked Raven.

'Sure,' said Lauterbach. 'They just ignored it. A couple of dudes without a care in the world. All Armstrong did was draw the curtains. I didn't get a chance to see inside the garage. The door was locked.'

'What kind of lock? Was it a Yale or a mortice?'

Lauterbach shrugged. 'A mortice, I guess. You know, the sort of lock you see on a door like that. I didn't pay that much attention.'

'What about the room overhead? Is there a separate entrance?'

'None that I could see.'

'Can you see the garage from the kitchen window?'

'Not unless they open the shades again.'

'I've got to get inside that garage,' Raven said quietly. He put the glasses in the glove-compartment and felt for his tools. 'I'll be back in a couple of minutes. Keep your eyes open.'

The return trip was easier now that Raven had his bearings. He kept to the strip of sodden grass that fringed the lane. The lamp was still out in the porch. A sliver of light showed through the shutters in the neighbouring room. He heard the sound of a television set and tiptoed round to the back of the house. The glow from the kitchen window extended across greasy cobblestones to the brick-built garage. The double doors were secured by an old mortice lock. A dropped-E master-key lifted the levers and he stepped into total obscurity. He held the torch over his head. The grey hatchback stood on the oil-stained concrete. He followed the light up the short flight of wooden stairs. The room was empty except for a truckle-bed with a pillow and blankets. Another blanket had been hung in the window. The room stank of mice. A comb lay on the bare boards near the bed. He held the torch closer. The comb was mock-tortoiseshell, the sort of thing a woman would carry. A few blonde hairs were trapped in the prongs. He put the comb in his pocket and locked the garage door behind him. The television set was still playing as he hurried back to the car. He wriggled behind the steering-wheel. 'They've got that hatchback in there. I got a look at the room. There's nothing there but a bed and some blankets. I found this on the floor.' He opened his hand on the comb. 'I think they've got Lucy Ashton.'

Lauterbach's face showed surprise. 'So what do we do?'

'Nothing,' said Raven. 'She could have been there and gone, there's no way of telling. But at least we've done what we came for. There's nothing more we can do now until Wednesday. We're going home, Hank, taking a well-deserved rest. You can bring Daisy over and we'll rustle up something to eat, have a nice relaxed evening.'

He turned the ignition-key. The engine came to life. He had a strong urge to get out of there fast.

Lauterbach fastened his seat-belt. 'Am I allowed to bring a couple of spliffs with me?'

Raven put the gears in reverse and started backing into the road. 'Why not? It'll probably do us good.'

Raven lay flat on his back on the couch, listening to the strains of a Mozart symphony, his eyes closed as it soared to its climax. Dope heightened his perception of sound, allowing him to track each instrument in the sixteen-piece orchestra. The music finished, he opened his eyes. It was an hour since they had finished their meal. An empty bottle of wine stood on the table between them. The Great Dane lay asleep on the floor, her nose pressed tight against the space at the foot of the door.

Lauterbach was shredding a mixture of Lebanese black and tobacco into a cigarette-paper. He licked the gummed edge and rolled the joint one-handed.

'I've had enough,' said Raven, yawning. 'I'm ready for bed.'

Lauterbach put the joint in his shirt pocket. 'You never told me about your place in Paris.'

Raven settled back again. 'It's at the top of a seventeenth-century building on Île-St-Louis facing the Seine. Kirstie inherited it from her brother.'

'How come you've never invited me?' asked Lauterbach.

'There's only one bedroom,' said Raven.

Lauterbach's expression was curious. 'Have you ever thought about living there permanently?'

Raven shook his head. 'Kirstie has, but this place has too many memories for me. You know how it goes. People get attached.'

The Great Dane stirred as Lauterbach shifted his legs. 'This business with Lambert could change your whole life.'

'It's happened before,' said Raven. 'You just have to make what you hope is the right choice. The rest is in the laps of the Fate Sisters. You've got as much chance with them as with anything else.'

'Let's hope they're listening,' said Lauterbach. 'I've got a feeling that once you're in Paris it'll be a long time before I see you again. I'm going to miss you, old buddy.'

It was the end of a long day and Raven was tired. He planted both feet on the floor and opened the door to the deck. The dog shot out, barking. Lauterbach collected the small plastic bag of hash.

'I've met a lot of guys in my time but you're something special. I want you to remember that.' His sincerity went far beyond the words. It showed in his eyes and handshake.

'Good night, Hank,' said Raven. 'Get a good night's sleep and I'll talk to you tomorrow.'

Tuesday came and went uneventfully.

Chapter Ten

The rented Honda was parked behind the closed filling-station on the corner of Grayshott Road. Raven sat at the wheel, Lauterbach beside him.

'Let's go through this again,' said Raven. 'I drop you off at the end of the lane. You get yourself to the back of the house where you'll have an idea what's happening inside. I'm betting that Lambert will be there. We don't know how he'll play it but I've got to get him to commit himself.'

Lauterbach stirred. 'That'll mean three against one. I'm not going to stand there and see you get your head kicked in.'

'It isn't going to come to that,' said Raven. 'Lambert knows that the bluffing is over. But he'll figure that I'm his main chance of getting his papers back. My guess is he'll make me some kind of proposition.'

A frown furrowed Lauterbach's forehead. 'That's a big house,' he objected. 'How will I know if you're safe?'

'All you've got to do is keep your ears and eyes open,' said Raven. 'If I feel in danger, I'll find some way of telling you.'

'Kick a window in,' said Lauterbach. 'I'll be right behind it.'

Raven looked at his watch. It was five to seven. 'If things go the way I hope, it shouldn't take long. You'll see me come out of the house. What you do is get back to the road and wait for me.'

'You've got a lot of balls,' Lauterbach said admiringly.

Raven set the car in motion and stopped on the grass verge at the end of the drive.

Lauterbach opened the passenger door and walked away. He was deep in the trees seconds later. Raven drove up the drive and stopped on the turning-circle in front of the house. The lamp in the porch was shining. A chink of light showed through the shutters of the room on the left. There was no sign of life in the rest of the house. The only sound was the wind in the treetops.

Raven loosened the belt of his Burberry and walked across to the porch. The front door was open. There was a phone on the hallway-table, a green baize door at the end of the panelled corridor facing him. 'Is there anyone here?' he called. His voice echoed back down the staircase. He peeped through the door on his left. The furniture was draped in dust-sheets except for two chairs in front of a television set. He walked down the corridor and pushed the baize door. A naked bulb hung on a cord from the ceiling, searching the crannies of the kitchen.

An old-fashioned cooking-range occupied most of the space in front of the end wall. A woman sat slumped on a chair with her head hanging. Vomit had caked on her Barbour jacket. Her knees were pressed close together. Armstrong and his brother-in-law stood near an open cupboard littered with crockery and cooking utensils. Armstrong was holding a small revolver.

Ludovic Lambert moved away from the curtained window, elegant in his dark Huntsman suit. His smile deepened the cleft in his chin. The woman flinched as he neared her.

'I don't think you two have met,' he said politely. 'This is Lucy Ashton, Mister Pinner.'

'What have you done to her?' asked Raven.

Lambert shook his head regretfully. 'She's a bit short-sighted without her contact lenses and she's tired and obstinate. She keeps insisting that she doesn't know where my property is. Maybe you'll tell her.'

A tile dislodged by the wind crashed on the cobble-stones outside. Raven widened his stance, his eyes fixed on Lambert. 'You seem to make a point of underestimating people. I know where your papers are, sure. But I certainly didn't bring them with me. You've still got to give me a signed affidavit.'

There was a certain grandeur about Lambert's self-assurance.

'I've decided to revise that arrangement. I want you to tell me the truth. If you have any difficulty about it, our friends here will be happy to refresh your memory.'

Raven found his voice. 'The police know where I am.'

Lambert clucked his tongue reprovingly. 'You wouldn't do that,' he said. 'What about Mallory? I'll ask you once more. Are you going to tell me where my property is?'

'No,' Raven said flatly.

Lambert's face hardened. 'You know what to do,' he told Armstrong. The baize door closed behind him.

Armstrong handed the gun to his brother-in-law. 'Watch him, Terry.'

He pulled a length of sash-cord from a drawer in the table and slashed it in two with a flick-knife. He was clearly enjoying himself.

'Up against the wall,' he ordered. 'And take your fucking clothes off!'

Raven backed off, holding his arms in the air. Then his shoulderblades touched the wall.

'Don't forget your shoes,' Armstrong added mal-evolently.

Raven saw that Armstrong was blocking the line of fire. It was now or never. He moved swiftly, planting a drop-kick in Armstrong's groin. Raven ducked low and reached for the light-switch, plunging the room in darkness. A shot rang out. The bullet ricocheted off the wall and smashed through the window pane. Raven flung the back door open and heard a car start up near by, footsteps pounding across the cobblestones. He found the light-switch again. Lauterbach was standing in the doorway with both hands wrapped around the butt of a stun-gun. Armstrong writhed on the floor. Terry lifted the revolver uncertainly.

'Drop it!' barked Lauterbach.

Terry's face set in defiance. Raven watched powerless as Lauterbach fired the stun-gun. The revolver clattered across the linoleum.

Terry rose on his toes like a diver leaving the high board. He posed, galvanized for a second, then pitched sideways like a stricken animal, his eyes wide and unseeing.

Raven stooped over him and checked his pulse and breathing. Both were unnaturally fast. He straightened his back. 'You had that bloody thing in your pocket all the time,' he challenged. 'Why didn't you stop Lambert, for God's sake!'

'Fuck him,' said Lauterbach, stepping over Terry. 'You're the one I was worried about.'

He took another look at Terry's recumbent body. 'He'll be all right.'

He put the stun-gun back in his overcoat and picked up the revolver from the floor. He shucked the bullets from the chamber and hurled them through the kitchen door. The revolver followed.

Raven took the length of cord and tied Armstrong's hands behind his back. He roped a noose around Armstrong's neck so that movement would throttle him and lashed him tight to Terry's unconscious body.

'We've got to get out of here fast,' he said. 'Give me a hand with her.'

Lucy's face was still stiff with shock, her voice barely audible. 'I can manage.'

They took her arms and supported her into the hallway. Raven gave Lauterbach the ignition keys. 'Get the engine going,' he ordered.

He lifted the phone on the table and dialled. There was a pause before a man's voice said, 'Fowler.'

Raven spoke distinctly. 'This has got to be short. I'm speaking from the Old Rectory, Grayshott Road, Hindhead.' He repeated the address. 'You'll find two people here who you should talk to. Lambert was here but I lost him. I'm going after him now.'

He put the phone down and hurried across to the car, the stink of burnt cordite in his nostrils. The headlamps were on, the engine running smoothly. Lauterbach was in the front passenger seat, Lucy wedged in the back behind him. Raven took the wheel and considered her. 'Where do you think Lambert would go?'

She moved her head helplessly.

'*Think!*' he urged. 'What about friends or family?'

She spoke in a thin bitter voice. 'He doesn't have any family or friends. Just the people he's used.'

'Well, rack your brains,' he said. 'There's got to be some place he'd go to.'

He headed the car along the A3. They drove thirty miles in silence, Raven constantly checking the rear-view mirror. The lights of a roadside restaurant came into view. Raven pulled on to the forecourt. There were a couple more cars and a truck parked near by. He switched the engine off and turned to Lauterbach.

'You could have killed that guy. It was crazy. Why didn't you warn me?'

Lauterbach showed no sign of compunction. 'You're one ungrateful sonofabitch. I saved your life in there. Have you thought about that?'

'I know what you did and I'm grateful,' said Raven. 'But don't ever pull another stunt like that on me.'

Lucy came out of her huddle, her face bleak in the lights from the restaurant.

'Don't you realize what I've been through?' she said angrily. 'The humiliation and torture! And you just sit there scoring Brownie points off one another. What about *me* for God's sake!'

136

Raven swung round on her. 'If it hadn't been for you we wouldn't be here. You're like Mallory. The only thing you think about is yourself.'

She glared at him short-sightedly. 'You don't like me very much, do you, Mister Pinner?'

'That's true,' he agreed. 'You're manipulative. A woman besotted by jealousy. And the name is Raven.'

She made a quick movement, hiking her skirt up, revealing the cigarette-burns that seared her tights to the soft flesh beneath.

'That's what Lambert did to me.'

'Jesus!' Lauterbach said feelingly.

'You'd better get yourself cleaned up,' said Raven. 'Can you make it inside?'

'I can walk and I can see,' she said. 'But I'll need some money. They took my purse away.'

Raven gave her a ten-pound note and some coins. Lauterbach reached back and unfastened the door. 'I'll stay in the car.'

Raven walked Lucy into the restaurant. There were a few people sitting at the tables, a self-service counter, a kiosk selling cigarettes and toiletries, a couple of pay phones. He pointed across at the toilets.

'Don't make it too long. Are you hungry?'

'Just something to drink.' She made her way carefully towards the Ladies. He watched until she was inside and bought two cups of coffee. He carried them to a table near the exit and lit a cigarette. What the hell was he doing here, anyway. The thought depressed him momentarily; then his mind reverted to Lambert. Instinct told him that Lucy could still help.

It was ten minutes before she returned, her face washed, her hair neatly brushed, the vomit sponged from the front of her jacket. She took a lipstick from the cheap purse she had bought and used a small mirror. Her make-up applied, she looked at him questioningly.

He pushed a cup across the table. 'Have you had any more thoughts about Lambert?'

'I don't *know* where he'd go,' she replied. 'If I did, I'd tell you.'

'What about his correspondence?' he said.

She put her coffee-cup down and wiped her mouth with a paper tissue.

'I handled most of it. All he kept was the personal stuff and that was always locked in his desk. I never even saw it. He was the only one with the key.'

The news lit a glimmer of hope for Raven. 'Wait here,' he said. He opened a phone-booth and dialled Mallory's number at the Danforth.

'No questions,' he said. 'Just listen. I've got Lucy Ashton with me. She's going to be staying with you for a few days. She'll tell you what's happened. I want you to get hold of a doctor in the morning and get him to look at her. We'll be there as soon as we can.'

He returned to the table, put his cigarettes in his pocket and spoke to her quietly. 'Have you got a lawyer?'

She glanced away, presenting an indifferent profile. 'A *lawyer*?' she mimicked. 'Why would I need a lawyer? It's Lambert who needs one, not me.'

He had a feeling that he was wasting his time, but continued. 'You'd better start facing facts. No matter how it all ends, there's one thing for sure. You're going to have to talk to someone who can give you the right kind of advice. In the mean time I'm taking you to Mallory's place. You'll be safe there as long as you do as you're told. You're in the same position as he is. Your best plan is to make peace with him, get your stories right.'

She turned the ends of her mouth down. 'Where is this place?'

'You'll know when you get there,' he said. 'What you've got to do is remember that it's your only chance to gain time. There won't be any left once the police get hold of Lambert.'

It was well after nine o'clock when Raven pulled up in

front of the Danforth Apartments. Mallory's windows were lit. Raven spoke over his shoulder. 'This is it.'

She gathered her few possessions, her face expressionless as they walked up the steps to the lobby. Raven rang Mallory's bell and the entrance clicked open. Mallory was waiting inside his room. His eyes fixed on Lucy as she came towards him. She stared at the bed, ignoring Mallory's hesitant greeting.

'Where's *he* going to sleep?' she said, turning to Raven.

His patience was nearing its end. 'Work it out between you,' he said, pushing her into the room and pulling the door shut. He sat in the car again, looking across at the windows. Lauterbach chuckled. 'I'd sure like to be a fly on the wall. Where do we go from here?'

'Home,' answered Raven. He left the car on the pub forecourt and led the way down the steps. Lauterbach sank on the sofa. Raven picked up the phone and called Jerry Soo's home number. 'Jerry, it's me. Have you heard?' he said.

'I just spoke to Fowler. They picked up those two guys from the house. They're talking their heads off. They're saying you used a stun-gun. Is that true?'

'It's true,' Raven said, looking at Lauterbach.

'Get rid of it,' snapped Soo. 'Where are you speaking from?'

'I'm at home.'

'What have you done with the woman?' asked Soo.

'She's out of harm's way,' said Raven. 'How's Fowler taking it?'

'I'm not too sure,' answered Soo. 'I'll know more when I see him. He's on his way up from Guildford. Does the name Foong ring a bell, students at the Wycherly Foundation?'

'I know them by sight,' said Raven. 'They're cousins.'

'The Immigration Squad took them off the plane coming in from Düsseldorf this afternoon. They were travelling on Hong Kong passports but their entry visas had expired. Their story is they thought they could get them renewed at the British Consulate in Düsseldorf. The only place they can do that is Hong Kong.'

'They know that already,' Raven said, puzzled.

Soo continued. 'The immigration people have been on the phone to Hong Kong, verifying the Foongs' applications for student visas. Both of them gave Lambert's name as their referee.'

'So?' said Raven, hunching a shoulder.

'There's a discrepancy in the dates,' said Soo. 'That's why they're being questioned. They're not saying a thing at the moment. Fowler's worried about the Met making the connection with Lambert. If they know that Fowler's concerned it'll complicate things.'

'I'm not with you,' said Raven. 'The Foongs don't *need* to talk. The worst that can happen to them is being put on the first plane back to Hong Kong, surely?'

'You're missing the point,' Soo said forbearingly. 'If the Met knows that another force is concerned, Fowler will have to declare his interest. It would be difficult to guarantee your anonymity.'

Raven stiffened. 'Let's get this straight,' he said. 'Are you telling me Fowler's going back on his promise?'

'No,' answered Soo. 'But he still has to protect himself. It's the reason I'm meeting him later. He wants to talk things over. Where are you going to be?'

'I've got to go out for a couple of hours,' said Raven.

'Call Fowler as soon as you're back,' said Soo. 'I'll probably be with him. It doesn't matter how late it is just as long as you phone.'

Raven replaced the receiver and sat beside Lauterbach. 'Did you get the gist of that?'

'Most of it.' Lauterbach was completely relaxed. 'We seem to be back to square one. Where do we go from here?'

'You've got to get rid of that stun-gun,' said Raven. 'It's dynamite. Once that's done, I want you to take the dog to Amanda's and stay there until you hear from me.'

Lauterbach looked at him narrowly. 'You mean you're dumping me?'

'It isn't a question of dumping,' Raven said gently. 'You've got nothing to reproach yourself with. I just have to be on my own from now on.'

'And that's it, is it?' said Lauterbach. 'You're not even going to tell me where you're going?'

Raven laid a hand on his knee. 'It's better for both of us. There's no alternative, Hank. I've got to do this on my own.'

'If that's the way you want it, old buddy,' said Lauterbach.

'It's the *only* way,' Raven answered.

Lauterbach heaved himself up and walked to the door. 'You've got Amanda's number. I'll be there if you need me. Just take care of yourself, hear now?'

The dog barked as Lauterbach approached the gangway. Raven closed the door regretfully, hoping that Lauterbach understood. He put his torch and the box of tools in his pocket. If all else failed he could always earn some kind of nefarious living. God knows he was getting plenty of practice. He crossed the Embankment and settled himself behind the wheel of the rented Honda. It was gone ten when he parked near the back gate to the Wycherly Foundation. He closed the gate behind him and walked up the driveway. Lights shone in most of the dormitory windows. The main building stood dark and deserted. There was no nightwatchman. The canteen staff came on duty at seven in the morning. He stood for a while on the empty car park, his gloved hand holding the small box of tools. A quick flash from the torch showed the well-worn lock on the front door. The skeleton key turned smoothly. He pulled the door shut gently and adjusted his eyes to the obscurity. Nothing stirred. He climbed the staircase, one hand on the banister-rail. The administration office was open. The key to Lambert's study had been left in the lock. He followed the narrow beam of light to the elegant desk. The lid resisted his pressure. He shone the torch on the tiny lock. He had no key that would fit. He took a sliver of surgical steel from his box, inserted the probe in the intricate mechanism and felt the lever move. Sweat was beginning to run down his ribcage. It was some time before the lock finally yielded. He lifted the lid and placed the torch inside, illuminating a yellow folder marked PRIVATE. He opened the folder and leafed through the contents. There was a two-page list of bank standing orders. Payments made for insurance, office furniture, utilities, vehicle hire, including the Bentley. There was a hand-written envelope addressed to Lambert. Raven read the letter inside.

Bowsprit Point Centre
Dock Street E14
(Telephone 071-295 0218)

11 February

Dear Ludo

I deeply regret having to inform you that a fire occurred here last week. Thank Heaven that no one was hurt! However the stairs to my flat were considerably damaged. I notified the Ajax Insurance Company (Willow Lane, SE11) and they sent a man to inspect the damage. He recommended a local firm of builders called Murphy & Sons. Their estimate for repairs amounted to £2050. Anyway, Ajax agreed the estimate and the work is in progress and should be completed shortly. It will take some time for the insurance money to come through. Meanwhile this is placing a severe strain on our slender resources.

Now comes the difficult part. You have been so generous over the years and I hesitate to ask for further favours. But would it be possible for you to tide us over our current difficulty? I shall understand if you feel unable to grant this request but *please* let me have your thoughts on the matter. It seems such a long time since you were here, Ludo. I would like you to see how your money is spent. Perhaps you could visit us soon?

With affectionate wishes,
Margery Gardner.

Lambert had scribbled a note in the margin: Increase S.O. from £1000 to £1500 per calendar month.

Raven pocketed the letter and relocked the desk on the folder. He turned off the torch and sat in the darkness. The letter was a dignified appeal for help from a woman on intimate terms with Lambert. The tone of her letter signified this was more than some chance business relationship. Raven kept a rein on his growing excitement and put himself in Lambert's place. This was no rudderless thief on the run. A man like Lambert would have access to false passports, alternative ways of leaving the country. Money would be no problem. What Lambert needed was a place where he'd be safe until word came that his escape route was ready. Somewhere that nobody knew about. The answer flashed clearly in Raven's head. He made his way out of the silent building and walked back to the car, unseen and unnoticed.

The return journey took thirty minutes. He backed the Honda in front his Orion. The Harley-Davidson had been removed from the cul-de-sac. A light burned forgotten in Lauterbach's cabin. Raven opened his sitting-room and poured a large whisky and water. He carried the glass to the sofa and took the phone in his lap. Fowler's number answered immediately. Traffic noises sounded in the background. Then a window was closed.

'I'm at home,' said Raven.

Fowler's country accent was slow and measured. 'Have you any idea at all what you've done? I wouldn't even have known that the Met was involved if it hadn't been for Jerry. Do you realize the position I'm in?'

'I do and I'm sorry,' said Raven. 'But with respect, I don't give a hoot about the Foongs and police politics. You gave me your word that I'd get the chance to find Lambert.'

'You had it,' said Fowler.

'Don't push me,' warned Raven. 'If you're going to renege on your promise, so be it. I'll just have to do what I think's right.'

Fowler's grunt was ominous. 'That sounds like a threat.'

'It's a statement of fact,' said Raven. 'I'm being realistic like you. I'm sick of this carnival ride. If things come to the worst, I'm going to call it a day, let you do the explaining and the hell with it.'

Fowler spoke patiently. 'There's no question of me breaking my promise. But this isn't *Alice in Wonderland*. The problem is knowing what you intend to do about Lambert.'

The letter from the Bowsprit Point Centre lay on the table, a talisman giving Raven fresh confidence. He took another leap of faith.

'I need three more days. If I can't come up with anything concrete by then you can do what you want.'

'OK,' answered Fowler. 'Let's assume that you find him. What happens then?'

'You make the arrest,' said Raven. 'All I want is to be there.'

'It's a deal,' said Fowler. 'But don't let him give you the slip again.'

'He won't get the chance,' Raven said grimly. 'The boot's on the other foot this time.'

'Good,' said Fowler. 'You can reach me on this number day or night. Whenever you need me. You want a word with Jerry before I hang up?'

'Just tell him I'll be in touch. And thanks for your support. I won't fail you, Commander, I promise.'

He read the letter from Margery Gardner and consulted the A–Z road map. He found Dock Street off Wapping Steps in a limbo of deserted wharves caused by the death of the river. He put the letter back in its envelope. No matter how the wheel spun it pointed at Lambert. He lifted the phone again and called the Carlyle Hotel. An operator connected him with Kirstie's room. She sounded surprised.

'That's weird,' she said. 'I was just going to call you. Hey listen, my flight's been confirmed. I'm on the Concorde on Sunday.'

His eyes sought the calendar. The dates crowded in on him. 'That's great,' he replied. 'I talked to Madame Bialgues. She's getting everything ready. I'll pick you up at Heathrow.'

'Are you excited?'

He took his gaze from the calendar. 'What do you think? It's lonely without you.'

Her voice was tender. 'We'll make up for it, darling. It's only another four days. If there should be a change in my schedule, I'll let you know in good time, OK?'

He put the phone on its cradle and walked to the bedroom. Everything he saw, touched or smelled reminded him of Kirstie. It was the last time, he told himself. But he still had to go through with it. He hit the thought hard. Tomorrow could mean an end to uncertainty. With any luck Kirstie would never know about it.

Chapter Eleven

It was an overcast day with Raven sitting behind the wheel of the Orion dressed in his chalk-striped blue suit and black brogues. He was waiting for Patrick O'Callaghan to leave his Upper Berkeley Street office. The lawyer emerged, dapper in his dark courtroom attire and carrying his briefcase. Raven removed his cap and Burberry and O'Callaghan sat down beside him.

'This had better be quick. I've got a lunch appointment with counsel at two o'clock.'

'Where?' asked Raven.

'The Royal Court Hotel and I don't want to be late,' warned the lawyer.

'I'll drive you there,' said Raven.

It was twenty-five past one by the clock on the dashboard. The lawyer lowered his briefcase resignedly. 'I do wish you wouldn't do this to me, John. We spent half an hour on the phone only yesterday. I thought I made my position perfectly clear.'

'You did,' said Raven. 'But it isn't as simple as that, is it? You're the one who sent Mallory to me in the first place. Remember?'

O'Callaghan made a quick gesture of disassociation. 'You could have said no. It wasn't as though you were under an obligation.'

'But you knew that I wouldn't. And you know what I told you yesterday. This is a lot more than a simple break-in. This is conspiracy, Patrick, abduction – and God only knows what else. I mean, the immigration people are involved.'

'Now wait a minute,' said the lawyer. 'Let's get something straight here. I knew nothing of fraud or for that matter of Ludovic Lambert except that it was his flat that was burgled. My advice to Mallory was the same then as it is now. To turn himself in and make a clean breast of things.'

Raven looked at him steadily. 'It's no good taking the high moral ground with me. Mallory's your responsibility.'

O'Callaghan's dark-blue eyes were wary. 'And you've put him in with Lucy Ashton – do the police know where they are?'

'No,' said Raven. 'Look, I'm not saying I didn't go into this with my eyes wide open. But a whole lot's happened since then and the thing is, I'm part of it.'

O'Callaghan sighed. 'I gave up trying to tell you what to do a long time ago. But I still think you should have warned me what you were up to.'

'That's because you didn't want to hear,' answered Raven. 'You did what you usually do: dump the whole thing in my lap and hope for the best.'

'That's unfair,' said the lawyer. 'I certainly didn't expect you to get involved in anything like this. I should have known better, of course. What about your own situation?'

Raven lifted his shoulders. 'The man in charge of the investigation has promised me immunity. He says my name won't even appear on the record.'

The lawyer frowned. 'And you believe him?'

'I believe Jerry Soo,' answered Raven. 'The guy's name is Commander Fowler, he's in charge of CID Guildford. He's just a couple of years from retirement. This represents a chance in a lifetime for someone like that. I spoke to him yesterday and we reached an agreement. He's given me three days to find Lambert.'

O'Callaghan's expression was dubious. 'Three days,' he repeated. 'And the man's on the run? What kind of proposition is that, for God's sake! It isn't even realistic.'

'No?' Raven smiled. 'And if I said there's a good chance that I know where Lambert could be, would that make it realistic?'

The lawyer sat straighter. 'Where?' he demanded.

'You'll know soon enough,' said Raven. 'If I'm wrong, I've agreed to let Fowler take over. I just want to be there when they bust him. Lambert's an evil, unscrupulous bastard. Mallory's the one to watch when it hits the fan. He and Lucy are trying to put the blame on one another at the moment, but Mallory's your problem. I don't know what sort of deal you can cut for him. You're the lawyer. But I warn you. Neither of them will be easy to handle.'

O'Callaghan's face was assured. 'I've no cause for concern on that score. I acted professionally.'

Raven glanced at the clock on the dashboard. 'Kirstie will be back on Sunday. We're spending Easter together in Paris.'

'Jesus!' the lawyer said feelingly. 'So what do you want me to do?'

Raven fastened his seat-belt. 'Remember this conversation for one thing. I don't want any more misunderstanding between us. I'm seeing this through to the end, Patrick. Put your seat-belt on or you'll be late for lunch.'

It took twenty minutes to drive to Sloane Square. Raven pulled up in front of the hotel. O'Callaghan opened the passenger door.

'When am I going to hear from you?'

'Just as soon as there's something to tell you,' said Raven.

He left the Orion in the cul-de-sac and walked east to Cadogan Pier. The next downstream ferry was due in twenty minutes' time and he was the only passenger waiting. He sat on the bench, his coat-collar up against the cold wind, his mind on O'Callaghan. His sole purpose had been to make sure that the lawyer knew how he felt about Lambert. Faced with unpalatable facts, his friend had a habit of retreating into a sort of moral vacuum, emerging only when the time came to discharge his responsibility with caution and probity. Raven had no doubt of the lawyer's friendship.

He disembarked from the ferry at Tower Bridge and followed the Embankment as far as Wapping Steps. A barbed-wire barricade blocked the way to deserted warehouses and empty wharves. He turned left past rusting cranes and oil-scummed water where ocean-going vessels had once discharged their cargoes. The noise of the open-air market grew louder as he approached the bottom of Dock Street. A row of covered stalls had been erected in front of the boarded-up houses. Some of the traders were dismantling their displays into pick-ups and handcarts. Asian women clad in saris scuffed through rotting fruit and vegetables making last-minute bargains.

A blank wall extended behind a dingy war memorial a hundred yards away. There was a café and a small public library on the left. The Bowsprit Point Centre was opposite, a long brown-brick building like a drill hall with a flat overhead. The entrance was open. Raven picked his way over waste ground to the back of the Centre. A narrow pathway protected by railings overlooked a finger of tidal water. There were four windows side by side at the rear of the flat. The only entrance was through the front door. He heard the sound of voices inside, the clatter of crockery. He retraced his steps to the pub at the bottom of Dock Street. The L-shaped bar was crowded with builders from a neighbouring site. Raven waited his turn to be served and carried his drink to a window table facing a wall defaced by scrawled graffiti.

A man spoke behind him. 'Makes you think, don't it?'

Raven swivelled his head. The man who had joined him was in his seventies wearing a stained reefer-jacket and lace-up boots. His face had a ferret-like look.

'Born and bred here, I was,' he announced. 'I seen a lot of changes in my time, I can tell you. We didn't have no Pakis or nig-nogs in them days, mate. We was all cockneys, then. People you could trust. Leave your street door open, you could.' He turned a jaundiced eye on Raven. 'You're not from these parts, I'll warrant.'

'That's right,' agreed Raven.

The man looked as though the news confirmed some inner suspicion.

'Well, watch yourself,' he said darkly. 'There's buggers out there what'll pick your pockets as clean as a whistle. And stick a knife in your gut if you try to argue.'

'I'll bear it in mind,' said Raven.

A nasal whine crept into the other man's voice. 'The old days have gone, mate. It's a bleedin' jungle out there. It ain't easy when you get to my age.'

He was clearly disposed to talk. Raven pushed his cigarettes across the table. The man made a sign of refusal. 'Do you live in the neighbourhood?' asked Raven.

'I told you,' the man replied. 'I was born no more than a half-mile away.'

'Then you must know where the Bowsprit Point Centre is,' Raven suggested.

The man's eyes grew cunning. 'It's at the other end of the street. Opposite the war memorial. Looking for Miss Gardner, are you?'

'I'm writing a book on the history of Wapping,' said Raven. 'There's a lot of research to be done. Someone said that Miss Gardner might be helpful.'

The man wiped his mouth on his sleeve. 'She ain't been here no more than twenty-odd years. All she can tell you is about the Old Age Pensioners. I used to play dominoes in there before I went to live with my daughter. What you need is someone who really knows the manor. I've worked every dock from here to Tilbury in my time. There ain't nobody knows Wapping better'n I do.'

Raven kept his voice casual. 'What sort of woman is she?'

'Miss Gardner?' The man pulled a face. 'She don't have

a lot to say to anyone, mate. They had a fire there a few months ago. She was lucky not to be burned to a bleedin' cinder, living alone like she does. She's a good enough woman but she can't abide people what drink. That's why she banned me.' He emptied his glass. 'She don't understand that you need something stronger than tea when you get to my age.'

'Is this your local?' said Raven.

The man nodded. 'I'm in here every day of my life, Sundays and holidays as well. But it don't get no easier, what with the price of a pint what it is.'

Raven gave him a handful of coins. 'Then I'll know where to find you,' he said, rising.

The man's fingers closed on the coins. 'All you got to do is leave a message behind the bar for Harry. I'll be here.'

Raven left the bar. A street-lamp illuminated the pay phone next to the Café. A group of elderly people was leaving the Bowsprit Point Centre, muffled against the cold. The entrance door closed behind them. Raven climbed the steps to the library and asked the girl at the desk for the electoral roll. There was only one name on the register. 2835, Gardner, Margery.

He looked up at the flat window. A silhouette showed behind the glowing curtains. There was no way of telling whether it was a man or a woman. Raven crossed the square in the gathering darkness. He put his ear against the crack in the door and heard movement upstairs. A thought struck him and he lifted the lid of the dustbin. An empty bottle lay on top of the refuse. He closed the lid gently, wondering what a teetotaller was doing drinking champagne. He looked across at the phone-box. If Lambert was there he'd be wary of answering calls. The empty bottle proved nothing. The woman could be entertaining a friend. It was not a time for rash judgement. But instinct outweighed reason. Lambert was in there somewhere, he was sure of it.

151

He sat in the café, a plate of bacon and eggs in front of him, eating with his eyes on the lighted window. Customers came and went as Raven maintained his vigil for the next hour. He pulled on his cap and turned left away from the square. He needed an excuse to get into the Centre without making Margery Gardner suspicious. He walked until a cab drove in sight with its light on. Raven lifted an arm. 'The bottom of Oakley Street in Chelsea,' he told the driver.

Raven went down the glistening steps to the gangway. The light in Lauterbach's cabin still burned. He unlocked the door to the sitting-room. He fixed himself a large Scotch and water and reclined on the sofa, reviewing the task in front of him. Ideas came and went, discarded. He took Margery Gardner's letter from his pocket and read it through again. He put the letter back in its envelope, sure now that he had the solution he needed. It would have to be properly timed. Late afternoon or early evening when the Centre was closed. He took a ringbacked notebook from a drawer and put it with the letter in his briefcase. Then he lifted the phone. Fowler answered his emergency number.

'I've got to see you,' said Raven. 'It's important.'

Fowler silenced the noise in the background. 'What's the problem?'

'I think I've located Lambert,' said Raven.

There was a marked pause before Fowler said, 'Where?'

'I don't want to talk on the phone,' said Raven. 'Can you come to the boat tomorrow morning?'

Fowler's voice was guarded. 'I've got a meeting with Jerry Soo at eleven. The Foongs are back in Hong Kong which means that the Met's lost interest. I could come by about ten if you like?'

'That's fine,' said Raven. He replaced the receiver, dismissing all thoughts of failure. It was a matter of playing his hunch, for better or worse.

*

It was a few minutes to ten on the following morning with the seagulls over head. Raven was wearing his chalk-striped blue suit and his hair had been brushed. He glanced around the sitting-room. The A–Z road map lay open on the glass-topped table; the coffee percolator bubbled in the kitchen. The buzzer sounded. Raven released the door at the foot of the steps and went to a window. Fowler walked along the deck, adjusting his gait to the sway of the boat. He was hatless, his heavy shoulders draped in a brown checked jacket over his yellow cardigan.

Raven waved a hand at the sofa. 'Make yourself comfortable,' he invited. He filled two breakfast-cups with coffee and sat down next to Fowler.

'Does our bargain still stand?'

Fowler sipped from his cup and put it down. 'Have you got any complaints?'

'No, but I'll give you my reasons for asking,' said Raven.

Fowler leaned back and listened, his pale-blue eyes fixed on Raven's face. He stayed silent until Raven had finished. 'You don't have a lot to go on, do you?' said Fowler. 'An empty wine bottle is hardly evidence. A talk with a drunk in a bar?'

'I *know*,' said Raven, tapping the side of his head.

'If you're wrong it could be highly embarrassing,' Fowler said gravely.

'I'm not wrong.' Raven's voice was determined. 'Just give me the chance and I'll prove it.'

'How do you propose to do that?' asked Fowler.

'By getting inside the flat.'

'It's a long shot at best,' Fowler said doubtfully.

'It's a certainty,' countered Raven. 'All you've got to do is pocket the winnings.'

Fowler closed his eyes briefly. 'And if you lose?'

'No problem,' said Raven. 'I tear up my ticket and leave things to you. Isn't that what we agreed?'

'And you're willing to take the risk?'

Raven ignored the cold light of reasoning. 'I have to,' he said. 'And you've got to help me.'

'What sort of help do you need?'

Raven put his hand on the map again. 'I don't know how long this'll take, but I won't make a move before late afternoon, say six at the latest. I want you to be where you can get to me fast when I call.'

Fowler thought for a moment. 'I've never been a gambler. But then I never met anyone like you either.'

'Does that mean you'll do it?' asked Raven.

Fowler offered a lopsided smile. 'You're an obstinate man. You've convinced me.'

'I know when I'm right,' said Raven. 'And I promise you won't regret it.'

'Let's hope so for your sake as much as mine,' said Fowler.

'Where will you take him?' said Raven.

Fowler shifted a burly shoulder. 'Guildford. I'll have someone with me.'

'Well, keep the car out of sight until you get the signal,' said Raven.

Fowler looked at his watch and hauled himself upright. The two men shook hands. Fowler fastened his jacket. 'It's a pity you and I never met a long time ago.'

'It wouldn't have worked,' Raven said, smiling. 'I'll see you tomorrow.'

He waited at the door until he heard the car drive away and drew a deep breath. All he needed now was a little luck.

Chapter Twelve

Lambert picked up his holdall and unlatched the gate to the short driveway. The two-storey Victorian cottage was built of weathered red brick with white-painted wood-work. A bracket-lamp illuminated the Citroën estate car parked under the chestnut trees outside the front entrance. The rest of the house lay in darkness. He rang the bell. The door opened immediately.

Caine was in his late thirties with a permanent suntan and eyes the colour of wet slate. He was dressed in jeans and a polo-necked sweater. He ushered Lambert into the silent hallway and waved a hand at the staircase.

'There's nobody here except us,' he said, reassuringly.

Lambert knew the house well. A single man, Caine lived as he pleased, spending most of his time travelling or in his darkroom.

Lambert followed his host through a door at the back of the house. Black drapes hung in the windows. An aerial photograph of farmland was propped on a retouching-frame under a hundred-watt spotlight. Boxes of 35mm film were stacked on a shelf beside a Hasselblad 150 camera and a vision enhancer. A map of the Channel between Dover and Calais lay open on the table.

He put the holdall on top of the map. 'Fifty grand. You can keep the bag.'

Caine took a brief look at the contents and locked the bag in a cupboard. 'I had a phone call from Herr Liede-mann this morning. I told him I hadn't heard from you.'

'Did he say what he wanted?' asked Lambert.

'He sounded worried,' said Caine.

Lambert moved an elegant shoulder. 'You did the right thing. Liedemann's going to have to take care of himself.'

'That's what I thought,' replied Caine. 'As I told you, your worries are over. Everything's set for tomorrow.'

Lambert sat on a chair. 'Tell me.'

Caine angled the spotlight. 'I've booked the two-seater Robin Trainer I always use. The flight shouldn't take longer than twenty minutes.'

'What about the weather?' asked Lambert.

'No problem,' said Caine. 'I checked with the Met Office. They said good visibility all day.'

'And radar?'

Caine's voice was patient. 'We've done a lot of business together. Have I ever let you down?'

'That's not the point,' Lambert insisted. 'We've never done anything like this before. I need to know these things.'

'I'm telling you,' said Caine. 'What you've got to do is relax. Leave me to deal with the technicalities. And forget about radar. I'll have my flaps down by the time we're over France. I'm booking out on an internal flight, remember. I've told them I'm doing a job for a property company interested in a site near Faversham. All I have to do is file an approximate flight plan and take off. It's as simple as that.'

A fresh doubt flared in Lambert's head. 'But you'll come back alone! Are you telling me no one will notice?'

Caine's sun-creased eyes stared with marked disapproval. 'You're beginning to piss me off with these stupid remarks. It's a flying club, not an international airport, for God's sake! The office is no bigger than this darkroom. You've got one guy in the control tower, a couple of flight instructors and a few mechanics out in the hangars. You won't even be noticed. Take a look at this.'

Lambert drew close as Caine pointed down at the map. 'Here's where I'm putting you down,' said Caine. 'An abandoned airstrip just east of Calais. A taxi will be waiting to take you to the station. You're on your own after that.'

Lambert straightened his back, relieved. Calais was no more than an hour's train-ride from Paris. Another two hours and he'd be in Basle.

Caine refolded the map. 'There's only one thing. You don't look like a photographer's assistant. I'll have to get you some gear. You can change back to your suit once we're airborne.'

Lambert moved his head in agreement. 'You seem to have thought of everything.'

'That's my job,' answered Caine. 'Making certain you get the sort of service you pay for. But there's something else I can tell you. I don't give a fuck where you go once you've landed, but I'll give you a piece of counsel. Stay well away from the Seychelles. The place is full of narks. They meet every boat and plane. You wouldn't last a day in that sort of company.'

The thought only bolstered Lambert's vision of freedom. 'I've no intention of going anywhere near the Seychelles.'

Caine looked at his watch. 'I've still got some phone calls to make. Where are you heading for now?'

'I'm taking a friend for a meal,' said Lambert.

Caine snapped off the lights. 'I'll give you a lift to Wimbledon station. There are always plenty of cabs out front.'

'Good man,' said Lambert, buttoning his overcoat, his confidence completely restored.

Caine took his car keys from his pocket. 'Nothing gets by you, does it, Ludo. That's why you came to me in the first place. I may be expensive, but I'm worth every penny once I go into action.'

'Every penny,' Lambert agreed, offering his quizzical

smile. 'Who knows – it could be the other way around the next time.'

Raven was sitting at a second-floor window of the Dock Street public library, watching the last stragglers leave the Centre, muffled and hooded against the bitter east wind. The entrance-door closed behind them and a light illuminated the curtains upstairs seconds later. The stallholders had cleared away the refuse and the street stood deserted in the waning daylight. Raven tucked his briefcase under his arm and pulled on his cap. It was cold outside after the warmth of the reading-room. A couple of teenage girls in the phone-box giggled as he crossed the square to the Centre. He put his thumb on the bell and waited. Footsteps descended the stairs. A middle-aged woman wearing a brown woollen dress and flat-heeled shoes appeared in the doorway.

Raven touched the peak of his cap. 'Miss Gardner?'

She tidied a wisp of soft grey hair and looked at him from deep violet eyes.

'That's right,' she agreed.

He took his notebook and pen from his briefcase and smiled politely. 'I'm from the Ajax Insurance Company. I wonder if I could have a few words with you?'

Her face cleared immediately. 'But of course. Do come inside.'

He wiped the soles of his shoes on the mat and stepped into the hallway. The Day Room was closed. He glanced at the stairs leading up to the flat. The carpet and woodwork were new, the walls freshly painted. He made a show of consulting his notebook.

'I'd better tell you why I'm here,' he said confidentially. 'The thing is, we've had some complaints about the builders. Are you happy with the work they did?'

Her expression was puzzled. 'Absolutely. It certainly wasn't me who complained. I thought they did an excellent job.'

'I'm afraid it's pretty much hit or miss these days,' he said, running his fingers lightly over the walls. 'You see, we know that Murphy and Sons have been sub-contracting some of their work and we value your account, Miss Gardner.'

She smiled at him demurely. 'Do you know this is the first claim I have made in twenty-two years?'

'I *do* know,' he said. 'That's one of the reasons we have to be sure we're taking proper care of you.' He put a hand on the stair-rail and lifted his head at the ceiling. 'The report I've got mentions extensive smoke damage. Do you mind if I take a quick look upstairs?'

'But there's nothing to see,' she objected. 'The surveyor you sent made a thorough inspection. He even took photographs.'

'I've seen them,' he said, sensing her reluctance. 'But I still have to make my own assessment. I can always come back another time if it isn't convenient. It's up to you.'

'No, no,' she said hurriedly. 'As long as it doesn't take too long. I have to go out later on.'

He followed her up the stairs to the flat. The two doors on the left of the landing were open.

'That's the kitchen and sitting-room,' she said and, indicating the door behind her, added, 'And this is my bedroom. You can see for yourself, there's no smoke damage here.'

He made a perfunctory inspection of the walls and ceiling and scribbled a note in his book. 'And that?' he said, pointing at the door beyond her.

She moved quickly, blocking his view. A faint flush showed on her cheeks. 'That's just the boxroom,' she said. 'I never use it.'

He smiled, convinced she was lying, and looked into the sitting-room. There were two cane chairs in front of the gas fire, a sewing-basket with skeins of knitting-wool.

He put the notebook back in his briefcase. 'Well, that

just about wraps it up. We'll send you a copy of my report for your files. I'm sorry to have troubled you, Miss Gardner.'

Her face was relaxed again, her gentle voice courteous. 'It's good of you to have come. I'm glad to know Ajax are so professional.'

'We do our best,' he replied, taking his cap from his raincoat pocket, certain now that Lambert was staying here.

She led the way down the stairs.

'Good night,' she said and closed the front door firmly.

The phone-box was empty. Raven crossed the square to the café. A few people were watching television. He positioned himself in the shadows behind the war memorial, keeping his eyes on the sitting-room window. The minutes dragged by. Then a taxi turned the corner and Lambert emerged. Margery Gardner let him into the hallway and the door closed quickly.

A rush of adrenalin poured into Raven's bloodstream. It was the moment he'd been waiting for.

He stepped into the phone-box and dropped a coin. Fowler's voice came on the line.

Raven had difficulty controlling his excitement. 'Where are you?'

'At the bottom of Dock Street,' said Fowler.

'Lambert's in the flat,' said Raven. 'Stay where you are, I'm on my way down.' He shouldered out of the phone-box and hastened along the empty street. The black unmarked Rover was parked near the pub with its lights out. Two men were sitting in front; Fowler was behind, wrapped in a sheepskin coat, holding the passenger door open. Raven moved in beside him.

'Did you see the taxi?'

Fowler cracked a mint in his molars. 'We've been here half an hour.'

There was a hint of omniscience in the way he said it that Raven found irksome. He looked at Fowler. 'I want to get Lambert out of there without any drama. He's got a woman up there. There's no point dragging her into it.'

Fowler shifted his ponderous weight. 'You're trying my patience,' he warned.

'Just a few minutes,' said Raven. 'I'll bring him out, I promise.'

Fowler turned to the man sitting next to the driver. 'What do you think, Joe? You've seen the back. Is there any way out?'

The man shook his head. 'There's a fifteen-foot drop. You'd have to be nimble.'

Raven's voice cracked with impatience. 'We're wasting time.'

Fowler glanced at his watch. 'OK. Do it. As soon as we see you're inside we'll be behind you. And don't disappoint me this time.'

Raven was already out of the car and trotting towards the square. The wind blew cold in his face but his body was fuelled with determination. The light still burned in the sitting-room window. He heard the sound of voices upstairs. He lifted the flap of the letter-box and called, 'Miss Gardner!' The voices stopped suddenly. He was on the point of ringing the bell when the door jerked open. Margery Gardner stared at him blankly.

Raven pushed by her and ran up the staircase. Lambert was standing in front of the open boxroom, his face stiff with shock.

'I should have known,' he said bitterly.

Margery Gardner moved to his side protectively. 'Shall I phone the police?' she said.

'Shut up and let me deal with this,' said Lambert, shoving her into the sitting-room. He took a briefcase from the bed behind him and gave it to Raven.

'Twenty thousand pounds. Just take it and go. No one will ever know.'

Raven jerked his hand at the sitting-room and put the briefcase on top of the desk. Margery Gardner was sitting bolt upright on a chair by the fire. She turned her head as a car stopped outside.

Raven kept his eyes on Lambert. The feeling of triumph had vanished, leaving his brain washed free of emotion.

'There are some people down there who want to see you,' he said. 'They're collecting a debt, the sort of debt that cancels everything else you owe. There's no need to involve this lady any more than you have done.'

Margery looked from Raven to Lambert, who ignored her. He buttoned his overcoat with a show of bravado. 'I'm ready when you are,' he said to Raven.

The two men descended the stairs. Fowler and the detective-sergeant were waiting outside the front door.

Lambert offered no resistance as hands impelled him into the back of the Rover. The man in the sheepskin coat beside him spoke with stilted formality.

'My name is Commander Fowler, Surrey Constabulary. You're being taken to Guildford Police Station for questioning. Do you understand that, Mister Lambert?'

The voice seemed to come from a great distance. 'I understand,' Lambert answered. Then a quick hope buttressed his courage. Maybe he could still do a deal of some kind. Turn Queen's evidence, give them chapter and verse about Liedemann, even Caine. Such things were possible.

'I'd like to speak to my lawyer before any interrogation,' he said.

'You've got the right to a phone call,' said Fowler. 'We'll take care of it when we get back to Guildford.' He signalled the driver.

The last thing Lambert saw, looking back as the car moved forward, was Raven standing at the sitting-room window.

Raven let the curtain fall and moved close to Margery Gardner. She seized his wrist and gripped it tightly. 'Where are they taking him?' she asked.

Her fingernails were digging into Raven's skin. He

freed himself gently. 'He's been arrested,' he said. 'You're going to have to face facts, Miss Gardner. He's in serious trouble.'

She shook her head and dabbed her eyes with a handkerchief. 'If only he'd told me, I might have been able to help.'

'There's nothing that you could have done,' he replied. 'He's just a crook at the end of his tether. That's something you'll have to learn to accept.'

She looked at him sadly. 'You don't seem to understand. He's my cousin, the only family I've got.'

Her despair moved him to compassion but the right words were difficult to find. 'He deceived you,' he said awkwardly. 'The way he deceived everyone who trusted him. Now he's out of your life. Is there anyone who could stay with you for a while?'

She answered with dignity. 'I have my faith, thank goodness. I don't need anything else.'

The briefcase was still on the desk. Raven had no idea if she had any inkling of what it contained.

He lifted his shoulders. 'I'm sorry it had to be this way.'

She pushed herself up from the chair. 'You're a kind man, whoever you are. But I'd like you to leave me alone.'

He walked down the deserted street, doing his best to erase her face from his memory. It was always the ones left behind who suffered the most. There was a cab waiting outside the Tower Hotel. He told the driver to take him to Chelsea. The lamps along the Embankment illuminated the boats and the windswept river. He let himself into the sitting-room with a feeling of despondency. Margery Gardner was still on his mind. He hung his coat in the closet and flushed her letter down the waste-disposal unit in the kitchen. He poured a stiff jolt of Scotch and water and checked the answering-machine. There was a message asking him to call New York at twenty-one hundred hours Greenwich Mean Time. It was twenty to nine. He sat in his favourite chair with his eyes on the clock, the whisky dissolving his apprehension. He reached for the phone as the second-hand nudged the hour.

Kirstie's voice was excited. 'Hi, listen! I can't stay long. I've got the woman waiting downstairs. I just wanted to tell you that I'm on the Concorde the day after tomorrow.'

The news rang in his head like a clarion-call. He finished his drink at a gulp. 'That's fantastic, darling! How did you manage it?'

'Pure luck. You wouldn't believe it. Somebody cancelled and I got the seat. And you don't even have to come to Heathrow. The agency's providing a limo.'

He saw her smile as though she were there. 'That's what I call service,' he said. 'When do you want to take off for Paris?'

'As soon as possible,' she said. 'I keep pinching myself. Imagine, four whole weeks together, darling!'

The thought fired his imagination. She was right. This wasn't something that *might* happen. It was now.

'I can't wait,' he said. 'I'll get the tickets tomorrow.'

'Bye-bye for now,' she said. She blew a kiss across the ocean and was gone.

The phone came to life as soon as he put it down. Jerry Soo spoke crisply. 'Congratulations! Fowler just called. The first thing is that he doesn't want any more direct contact with you until the case is over. Lambert's appearing in court in the morning. Fowler says you'd do better making yourself scarce for a while. It'll be better for everyone.'

'Suits me,' said Raven. 'What's he going to do about Margery Gardner?'

'He'll have to take a statement from her but I wouldn't worry about it. He says she's gone through enough as it is.'

'I'm taking Kirstie to Paris,' Raven said calmly. 'As far as she's concerned, none of this ever happened.'

'Well, be careful,' warned Soo. 'I've got a lot on my plate at the moment and I doubt if I'll be able to see you before you take off, but I'll call you and keep you posted.'

'Do that,' said Raven.

He refilled his glass, put a record on the stereo system, and doused all the lights. Then he sat in the darkness, listening to Sinatra sing Johnny Mercer. The voice and the melodies carried him three thousand miles. He heard the record through and made himself ready for bed. The woman he loved would soon be home.

Chapter Thirteen

It was the following day. Pale sunshine dappled the sitting-room curtains with the promise of spring. Raven was still in his robe and pyjamas. He reached for the telephone. Mallory's tone was as bleak as wind blowing across the tundra.

'It's just as well you called. I've decided to turn myself in. I can't live any more like this.'

'Where's Lucy?' asked Raven.

'She's still in bed,' said Mallory. 'Did you hear what I said?'

'I heard,' said Raven. 'Does Patrick know about this?'

'He's going with me,' said Mallory. 'I'm meeting him in his office at eleven o'clock.'

'Let me talk to Lucy,' said Raven.

There was a murmur of voices; then she came on the line. 'I told you before,' said Raven. 'You need a lawyer.'

'I don't *know* any lawyers,' she wailed. 'Can't you help me?'

'No,' he said flatly. 'You're on your own now. I'm out of it. Your best bet is to see if Mister O'Callaghan can help. You'll have to talk to him yourself.'

He replaced the receiver, giving her no chance to reply. The phone rang again ten minutes later. 'I've just talked to Mallory,' said Patrick O'Callaghan. 'I've been in touch with Chelsea CID. I've arranged to surrender him. Lucy Ashton's coming as well.'

'Are you happy with that?' asked Raven.

'There's no reason why not,' said the lawyer. 'They're co-defendants, after all. What's the position with Lambert?'

'He'll be in the Guildford Magistrates' Court this morning.'

O'Callaghan thought for a moment. 'I may have to ask for a severance, a separate trial. It all depends what they do at Chelsea. I don't even know if they'll prefer charges. They'll probably leave that to Guildford.'

'As long as you don't count on me any more,' warned Raven. 'Kirstie and I are spending Easter in Paris.'

'The best thing you could do,' said the lawyer. 'How much does she know about any of this?'

'Nothing,' said Raven. 'And that's the way it's got to be.'

'Well, give her our love and enjoy yourselves,' said O'Callaghan.

'We shall,' Raven said with confidence.

Mrs Burrows appeared shortly afterwards. He told her of Kirstie's new plans. He spent the rest of the morning buying the tickets for Paris and French francs from his bank. He finished his lunch and browsed for a while in Hatchards, selecting some books to read on holiday. It was a strange feeling, finding himself with time on his hands after the cut and thrust of the last two weeks. He bought a large bunch of freesias for Kirstie and returned to the *Albatross*. Lights glowed in the spotless sitting-room. Mrs Burrows had left a welcome-home card on the table. Raven put the flowers in a vase and placed them next to Kirstie's photograph. He went through each room, ensuring there was nothing that might arouse her curiosity. Then he closed the curtains and watched videos until he was ready for bed.

It was the morning after Kirstie's arrival. They had eaten in *Wielka Polska* the night before, a candle-lit table between them. Kirstie had done most of the talking, rethreading the gap in their lives. He hadn't been taking proper care of himself, she chided. He looked terrible. He was fine, he told her. It was being alone that did the damage. They walked home hand in hand like a pair of teenagers, content with each other's company.

Now he sat in his chair wearing his brass-buttoned blazer, grey flannel trousers and loafers, waiting for Kirstie to finish her packing. His own bag stood by the door with an Air France label tied to the handles. A newspaper lay open on his knees. The article was headed:

SURREY MAN CHARGED WITH FRAUD

Ludovic Lambert, 58, giving an address in Hollywood Mews, SW10, made a brief appearance before Guildford magistrates today. Lambert, Principal of the Wycherly Foundation in Corton Bassett, Surrey, was charged with two counts of fraud and one of false imprisonment. Jeremy Loder, QC, for the Crown, told the magistrates that further charges would be brought including immigration offences. Three men and a woman were being held in connection with the matter. The court would hear evidence that Lambert conspired with a German national to provide false references for Hong Kong residents seeking to enter the United Kingdom on student visas. Henry Porter, QC, for the defence, said that his client strenuously denied all charges and pleaded Not Guilty. The magistrates rejected an appeal for bail and remanded Lambert in custody for fourteen days.

He put the newspaper down as Kirstie came through from the bedroom. The lemon-coloured linen suit she was wearing heightened her suntan. Her hair had been styled in a *gamine* cut and she looked radiant. She put her bag down next to his. 'Have you got the tickets?' she asked.

He tapped the inside pocket of his blazer. 'You'd better get a move on. The cab'll be here any minute.'

'Good,' she replied. 'I want to get out of here before Mrs B shows up.'

The phone rang as she walked back to the bedroom. Raven's fingers closed on the receiver.

Lauterbach's voice was tense. 'Have you read *The Times* this morning?'

'Yes,' Raven said hurriedly. Kirstie was coming down the corridor, carrying her velvet beret and camel-hair coat.

'I can't talk to you now,' Raven said. 'We're on the point of leaving for Paris. We'll see you when we get back.'

He lifted his head at Kirstie. 'Hank,' he explained. 'He's staying with Amanda for a couple of days, getting his laundry done and stuff.'

She threw her coat on the sofa and nodded indifferently. She took the newspaper from the table before he could stop her and scanned the article. 'That's something I'll never understand,' she said, shaking her head. 'A man like that in a position of trust. What on earth makes them do it, John?'

He folded the newspaper. 'Who knows? Greed, I suppose.'

She took his face in his hands and looked deep in his eyes. 'At least I don't have to worry about you any more.'

'You never did,' he said, smiling up at her.

She released him reluctantly. 'You're an old rogue,' she said fondly. 'But I love you the way you are.'

The door-buzzer sounded. 'That's the cab,' he said quickly.

He helped her on with her coat and picked up the bags. They walked out on deck. He took one last look at the trees across the river. There was nothing that held him here now, but he still had a pang of nostalgia.

'Well, come on,' Kirstie said impatiently. 'We don't want to miss the plane.'

He followed her up the steps to the waiting taxi, sure that wherever she went he would be there beside her.